ROGUE WAVE

The Inland Seas Series - Book 2

GWYN MCNAMEE

Rogue Wave
by Gwyn McNamee © 2019

Cover Design: Michelle Johnson at Blue Sky Designs
Cover Models: Zack Salaun and Bahar
Photographer: Wander Aguiar
Editing: Proofing With Style

There are always waves on the water. Sometimes they are big, sometimes they are small, and sometimes they are almost imperceptible. The water's waves are churned up by the winds, which come and go and vary in direction and intensity, just as do the winds of stress and change in our lives, which stir up the waves in our minds.

Jon Kabat-Zinn

Acknowledgments

There are never enough words to thank the people who help me get my books ready for publication. My husband supports me completely and helps in any way he can when I'm stressed out and trying to finish a book - whether it is a bottle of wine or bourbon, a few hours of quiet work time while he takes our daughter out on an adventure, or a good vent session. I can't thank him enough for all he does.

To my amazing beta readers and my super alpha reader, I literally could never do this without you guys. You help me see the flaws in my own writing and make them better.

Again, a thank you to Jacquelyn Burton and Catherine Horn Gianelloni - your expertise on all things maritime has been invaluable. Thanks for helping me assure these stories are as accurate as possible.

ONE

Cutter

The four men sitting around the table couldn't be more completely fucking oblivious to me watching. Laughter and jokes float through the summer afternoon air while they eat more food than I thought humans were even capable of ingesting in one sitting.

I guess it's true...Italians love to eat.

My stomach gurgles.

Maybe I should've taken E up on his offer of breakfast before I left this morning instead of eating a protein bar on the way here. One of his big spreads would have tasted a lot better and filled me up for the endless hours of surveillance. As it stands, I'll be stopping for a massive meal once these assholes settle in for the night and I can head out of Chicago and back toward the warehouse.

Milo lounges on the grass next to the bench with his face resting on the top of my foot. He releases a heavy sigh. I glance down at him. He raises his eyebrows and stares back up at me as he offers a low whimper.

Demanding little shit.

I reach down and scratch the top of his head. "I know,

boy. Just a little while longer. We'll have E make you some-thing special when we get home. I promise."

Work has to come first today.

I reach into the paper bag next to me and grab two treats. Milo rises on his back paws and snatches them from my hand. That will appease him long enough. They can't be here much longer. It's already been almost an hour since they sat down for lunch.

A train rattles by on the track between where I sit in Monument Park and the focus of my attention, obscuring my view of Moretti's patio and my targets. This location certainly isn't ideal for recon, but it's as close as I can get and still remain inconspicuous. The park and Milo give me the perfect cover to watch my prey, even if I do lose my line of sight for a few seconds a couple of times an hour.

The metal monstrosity passes, once again revealing the Marconis and their henchmen.

One goon stands outside the door to the patio, blocking anyone else from coming out, even the servers. They hand off food to him, and he lumbers over and sets it on the table. A strikingly tall, thin woman with long, sleek black hair in a dark suit that hugs all her perfect curves stands like a gargoyle sentinel behind the table where *Il Padrone,* his *capos,* and Arturo eat.

It's the first real chance I've seen to get the job done. When Warwick gave me the okay to take *Il Padrone* and Arturo out, I knew it wouldn't be an easy task.

This has to be done delicately so the innocent don't get hurt and the hit can't be traced back to us. Surveillance on them over the last week hasn't presented many opportunities for me to take them out.

But here…at this restaurant…this lunch spot…it's a perfect set-up.

Between the church behind me, the train station immediately to my left, the parking lot, the Edison Park Bowling Alley, and restaurant building next door to Moretti's, and the park I'm currently in, I have any number of places to set up with my rifle. They'll be dead, and I'll be long gone before anybody even realizes what happened.

God, please let this be a regular lunch place for them.

It's the first time I've followed them here since I started planning the hit, but *Il Padrone* seems to be a creature of habit. If this turns out to be his regular Friday lunch spot...I'm golden. Between now and next week, I'll gather more intel on the area. By then, I'll be ready.

Game fucking on.

My fingers practically itch for it.

The Marconis have been a thorn in all our sides for far too long. After what Arturo did to Warwick and Grace, it became clear that things are only going to get worse the longer we're under their thumb. Arturo is making moves. He has his sights set on *Il Padrone's* powerful seat, and it's only a matter of time before the old man croaks or retires and hands it right over to him.

That would be disastrous for all of us.

Rather than sit back and wait for things to go to fucking hell, through months or even years of being jerked around by Arturo while *Il Padrone* struggles to maintain control, we're taking action. *I'm* taking action.

Maybe we should have done it sooner. Five years of this has been five years too many. But we never expected it would come to this—hijacking ships that are transporting drugs. There are a lot of things the guys will put up with—guns, theft, and violence being the least of them—but after what War went through with his father, drugs are where we draw the line.

It should have been where *Il Padrone* drew the line, too. It's inconceivable he's still keeping Arturo so close after what he did...unless he still doesn't know everything or is turning a blind eye because Arturo is his nephew and heir apparent. Regardless, the two sure look pretty damn chummy based on what I've seen the last week.

They're practically inseparable. As if Arturo never went behind his uncle's back.

It doesn't make any sense.

But why *Il Padrone* does what he does is irrelevant at this point. He sealed his fate a long time ago when he made his deal with Warwick. It's just taken until now for War to finally realize it's time to end all this.

That's the one good thing Grace has brought to him —clarity.

It doesn't matter that we've gotten away with it for the past five years. It doesn't matter that we enjoy it most of the time, that the violence and adrenaline fill a different void each of us has in our lives. It's gone on for too long. We're too exposed. Being at the beck and call of someone like *Il Padrone* has been risky since day one, but being at the beck and call of a man like Arturo would be a true death sentence. We can't sit around and wait for him to take over.

Ending things now is the only way we all walk away unscathed.

I flip a page in the book on my lap without taking my focus off the Marconis. One benefit the glasses provide...they make it a hell of a lot easier to conceal the direction I'm looking. I glance down at Milo again, then back up at the restaurant patio.

My heart leaps into my throat, and I fight the urge to whip my head around and search.

She's gone.

The beautiful, stoic woman who has been glued to *Il Padrone*'s side since the moment I started following him is no longer standing guard on the patio.

Where the fuck did she go?

It couldn't have been more than three seconds that I looked away. I reach down to pet Milo and use the opportunity to casually scan the surrounding sidewalks, the parking lot, and the street that separates the restaurant from the park where I sit.

A couple strolls hand in hand down to the right of the lot. A white Prius turns the corner and makes its way down Oldsted Avenue toward Moretti's. A black SUV makes the same turn, but there's no sign of her.

I turn to the left toward the train station. If she crossed the street in my direction, the building would give her a perfect cover.

Shit.

Maybe she only went into the restaurant for something, but a familiar tingle slides up my spine. One that's been a warning system for as long as I can remember. One that's always kept me alive, even in the worst situations. One I ignored just long enough to almost pay the price once. It's not a mistake I'll make again.

I slowly close the book and set it on the bench beside me. I shift my hand to my side so it's closer to where my Glock sits in the holster on my hip.

Something's not right.

Arturo rises to his feet from where he was seated next to *Il Padrone* and leans down to whisper something in his uncle's ear. *Il Padrone* chuckles, and Arturo slaps him affectionately on the back before turning and strolling toward the door into the restaurant.

Fuck. Now where is he going?

The goon blocking the door moves to the side and allows him to enter. *Il Padrone* laughs and jokes with his *capos* as dread claws at my gut.

Milo climbs to his feet and whimpers. He senses it, too.

Shit.

The Prius turns into the parking lot for the train station,

and the black SUV's engine roars. It speeds up, and a cacophony of gunshots ring out, breaking the tranquil silence of the beautiful summer afternoon. I pull out my gun, grab Milo, and dive behind the bench.

But the bullets aren't directed my way.

The patio explodes as it's decimated with automatic weapon fire.

Il Padrone and his *capos* dive for cover, but it's too late.

Like knocking over dominoes, they fall one by one...

Frank Braone. Angelo Carozza. Michael Grasso. And finally, *Il Padrone*. The bullets wrack his body. He drops to knees, then tumbles backward onto the concrete with his men. The man at the door there to protect them crumples right along with him.

Holy shit. Fuck. Fuck. Fuck.

The SUV roars down the street. Tires squeal as it rounds the corner, and I get one last glance at it before it disappears.

No license plate on the back.

Of course.

If you're going to take out the Marconis, you don't do it in a way that can be traced, which is precisely why I've been biding my time, waiting for the perfect opportunity.

Looks like someone beat me to the punch.

There's another player.

Warwick isn't going to be happy about this. My hand tightens around my Glock, and I ease it back into the holster.

The last thing I need is to be seen with a weapon after what went down. What I need is to get the hell out of here before the cops arrive and start asking questions. I can't be associated with this in any way. No one can ever know I was here.

"No!" The cry comes from my left near the far side of the train station.

I tense as the mystery woman who has been *Il Padrone's*

shadow lately darts across the street from near the train station toward the patio.

She *was* over here. Too close for comfort.

Why? Why the hell did she leave him? Why the fuck did Arturo get up right before the attack?

It's all a little too coincidental to be an accident.

She leaps over the low iron railing around the patio and drops to her knees beside *Il Padrone*.

Even from here, across the street with a parking lot and train tracks between us, watching her hand shake when she reaches out and presses it against one of the wounds on his chest sends a familiar pain spreading through my body.

The explosions still ring in my ears even after six years.

As do the echoing screams.

The disorder and confusion tighten my chest as much today as they did then.

And the pain…

I squeeze my eyes shut against the memory, then force them open. This isn't the time or the place to fall back into that dark hole. My focus needs to be completely on what's unfolding in front of me.

The woman leans down closer to *Il Padrone*, her face mere inches from his own. Someone from inside the restaurant shoves open the door to the patio and rushes over to them. He kneels next to the woman, and she glances over her shoulder toward me. Fathomless amber eyes meet mine.

Shit.

That's my cue to leave. I rise to my feet, grab the book I borrowed from Warwick off the bench, and casually walk from the park toward where I parked several blocks away.

Sirens scream in the distance, but I continue my slow stroll away from Moretti's and the bloodbath. Running would draw attention—the last thing I need right now. Even though I wasn't involved, my name in the police reports or newspapers connecting me in any way with the Marconis would be like painting a goddamn bullseye on the crew.

She looked right at me. She saw me and *knew* I was there. Which means even if I didn't pull the trigger, I'd be a suspect. She'll either rat me out to the police or come looking for me herself.

This all went to shit in the fucking blink of an eye.

That seems to be happening a lot lately.

TWO

Valentina

I stumble out of the cab with tears blurring my vision, but they can't stop me from seeing the blood covering my shirt and pants and staining my hands despite the fact that I've washed them.

Il Padrone's blood.

The man who begged me to help him. The man I swore to protect. The man I promised would never be touched as long as I was watching his back.

I failed.

He's dead...

They're all dead...

All the people he trusted most, gunned down in one fell swoop. A bloodbath on a sunny Friday afternoon.

The cab pulls away, and I drop to my knees on the sidewalk in front of *Il Padrone's* mansion and retch. Bile climbs up my throat and splashes against the cement. I repeatedly heave until there's nothing left in my stomach as the day's events replay in my head on an endless loop. Every single detail flashes in perfect clarity.

The bright sunlight...

The mouth-watering scent of the food...

The clanking of the train when it passed...
The laughter of *Il Padrone* and the men...
The gunshots...
The blood...
How could this have happened?

I was so careful. I watched him like a hawk. No one got near him, and he didn't go anywhere without me clearing everything first. He knew that lunch was a bad idea. I told him, but the stubborn old *mulo* didn't listen. Twenty years of eating Friday lunches at Moretti's made it the easiest and most obvious place to take him out. But he was too damn stubborn to change his routine.

He paid the ultimate price.

And the guy sitting on the bench across from the restaurant must have had something to do with it.

He was there for over an hour with his dog and a book in the middle of August in Chicago. It was sweltering today, far too hot to want to sit out in the sun for that long. And if that wasn't suspicious enough, even with the mirrored aviator sunglasses covering his face, I could feel his eyes on me, on the man I was supposed to guard.

It's why I abandoned my post to cross the street to check him out. Something about it was all wrong. He wasn't just out enjoying the beautiful sunshine. He was there for another reason.

Oh, my God. I was so stupid.

He was the decoy.

He was there to draw me or *Il Padrone*'s other security away from the patio so the shooters would have a clean line of sight at him. And that's exactly what happened. I left *Il Padrone* to check out the potential threat.

Without me there, he was a goddamn sitting duck.

By the time I saw the SUV from where I stood on the backside of the train station across from the restaurant, it was too late. The gunfire was already tearing the patio apart.

Even now, almost ten hours later, it feels like only seconds ago. I can still feel his blood pouring through my fingers as I desperately tried to keep it in him.

The shaking of my body and the heaving keep me prone for what feels like hours, but eventually, the retching stops long enough to climb shakily to my feet and stumble to the front door of the mansion.

It's the only place I could think to go. The only place that's been a home since I arrived here.

I need answers. Like why Arturo got up to use the bathroom right before the shots.

Was it just a coincidence, or was it a calculated move by that weasel?

Il Padrone didn't trust him, and I don't either.

"Watch your back, tesoro…"

Those blood-choked words *Il Padrone* whispered to me before he took his final breath will never leave me. He suspected what I'm now sure is true. Arturo was involved in this. He may not have pulled the trigger, but he paid someone else to. Maybe the man across the street was his spotter, the one who called the shooters to tell them to come once Arturo left the kill zone. Or maybe he was simply a distraction to lure me away long enough for them to take *Il Padrone* out.

Too many unknowns. Too much blood. No one I can trust.

I need to get to *Il Padrone*'s office. If he found anything to incriminate Arturo since we last spoke about it a few days ago, to prove what he suspected about deals and moves happening behind his back, it would be in the office at the mansion. It's the only place he conducted business recently. He didn't trust that Arturo hadn't bugged the main offices, and he had me check this one at home three times a day. If I had done that at the salvage yard, Arturo would have seen me and known *Il Padrone* suspected him. That would have made my being here to investigate covertly useless.

It's hard to catch a rat when he knows you're setting a trap.

My hand shakes as I pull my keys from my pocket. I manage to get the right one into the lock and twist it open. The heavy oak door resists my push for a second before finally giving way. I stumble into the foyer of the house that, only hours ago, I stood in with *Il Padrone*—alive and well.

God, has it only been a few months since I first stepped over this threshold?

So much has happened in such a short amount of time.

"Valentina?" Tony jumps to his feet from the chair in the foyer facing the door. "You're here…" His dark eyes roam over my blood-stained clothes and hands and finally meet mine. "We weren't, uh, expecting you."

I swipe at the tears on my cheeks. I can't let this *deficiente* see me cry. No weakness. These men never respected me or thought I could do their job when I was brought on, and I'm not about to give them fodder for their sexist beliefs now even with *Il Padrone* dead because of my failure.

"Where the hell else would I be? *Il Padrone* is dead."

He glances to his left, down the hallway toward *Il Padrone's* office and nods. "I know. We got the call."

Call? What call?

"From whom?"

No one else came to the hospital. I rode alone in the ambulance with the man who was my responsibility. His own nephew, his heir apparent, never even bothered to show up. Not a damn word from him, not even a phone call, after he got up and walked into the restaurant right before the shooting.

Tony presses his lips together in a firm line. He's one of Arturo's cronies. I'm not going to get answers from him. He's just the muscle, anyway. And if he's here, it means Arturo is milling around somewhere close. I brush past him and storm down the hall toward *Il Padrone*'s office. Somehow, I know Arturo will be there. *Il Bastardo.*

Arturo's deep voice hits my ears halfway there, sending a chill over my skin. By the time I reach the open door, other voices mingle with his, voices I know all too well.

I step into what's clearly a meeting. One I wasn't invited to. In fact, no one has tried to contact me since the shooting at all.

What's left of *Il Padrone's* crew, who were mysteriously unavailable for today's lunch, stand in front of the desk with a line of random, unfamiliar goons to the side.

Arturo occupies the place of honor on the other side of the massive piece of carved wood furniture where his uncle sat for years. His almost-black eyes meet mine. The man remains stoic, but he doesn't seem surprised to see me. "Valentina, when did you get here?"

That's the question he has for me?

Not what happened? Not if I saw who did this?

"I just left the hospital. I came straight here. What the hell is going on?"

He lifts his hands and shrugs. "I thought that would be obvious. I'm talking to my *capos.*"

"Your *capos?*"

A cool grin spreads across his face. "Of course. We received the bad news that my uncle passed away and thought it best to get the ball rolling right away."

Who told him about Il Padrone's *death?*

There was no one else left—no one but me. Unless someone from the hospital is on Arturo's payroll, or he had someone following me after the shooting.

Both are possible.

And it seems Arturo is stepping right into the shoes so recently vacated at the head of the Marconi family.

I squeeze my eyes shut against the tears and try to process what he said.

"Get the ball rolling..."

"What ball rolling?" I take in the faces of all the men in the room, and something cold and sinister slithers up my spine.

In the few months I've been in Chicago since I got the desperate call for help, I've been watching everyone carefully, trying to weed out the snakes in the grass *Il Padrone* was so certain existed within his organization. Some of these men have been on my radar from the beginning; others, I would never expect to see here with the man sitting in that chair— the chair *Il Padrone* ruled this area from for decades.

He's always been the number one snake on my list.

Arturo gives me a cool once-over. "I'm glad you could join us, Valentina. There are going to be some changes made to the organization, and it's important that everyone is on the same page."

Changes?

Acid churns in my stomach, and the men in the room avert their eyes from mine.

I clench my blood-stained fists at my sides. "What kind of changes?"

Arturo reclines casually and steeples his hands in front of his mouth. "First, your services will no longer be needed."

It isn't a surprise. He never wanted me here, but if he thinks he can send me back home after what just happened, he has another thing coming. "I came from Italy for this job, for *Il Padrone*. I have no intention of leaving."

Until I've avenged his death.

He sneers at me and leans forward to rest his arms on the desk. "My uncle wanted you here. I do not. I can't trust you to get on board with the new direction of the business."

Any direction Arturo plans on taking the Marconis is a bad one. *Il Padrone* knew that and dreaded the day his nephew would take over.

Arturo nods toward his new captains. "We will be stepping

into the drug trade with both feet. My sources in Lecce assure me it'll be no problem to obtain shipments and create a pipeline."

Porca puttana!

He's insane and even more dangerous than we thought.

The cartels have a firm stronghold on the drug trade in this town. The last thing he should be considering is trying to infringe on their territory. He already made a terrible decision when he sent Warwick and his men out after someone else's shipment behind *Il Padrone*'s back. To formally move into the business, to set up a new pipeline, that's a major statement. One that won't be taken lightly by those in control of the cartels.

Il Padrone would never have allowed it. Not in a hundred years. Not in a million. He was furious when he learned what Arturo had done. It was the straw that broke the camel's back and convinced him his distrust of Arturo was warranted.

If only he'd listened to me...

If only I could have protected him...

I shake my head and hold his stark gaze. "You can't be serious. You can't just—"

He holds up a hand to silence me. "I think it's best to go back to the mother country, Valentina. There is no place for you here. Go home to your *family*."

The emphasis he puts on the word *family* has that dread already wrapped around my spine now crawling into my throat. I swallow through it and shiver.

It suddenly feels like I have a giant bullseye painted squarely on my back.

THREE

Cutter

W arwick is on me the second I push open the door to the warehouse.

"So?" He stands with his hands on his hips and raises dark eyebrows at me. "What did you find out?"

I scowl at him before I squat to unhook Milo's leash from his collar. He trudges off for the kitchen, undoubtedly, to look for any little morsels that may be on the floor, or to see if someone refilled his food bowl. I rise and wrap the leash around my hand.

"We have a problem."

There was no way I was going to call the guys to let them know what happened. Too risky if anyone ever tracked my phone or was listening in on them or me.

War frowns. "Something other than the problem we already know about?"

"A much bigger problem." I push past him and make my way across the warehouse. He follows, and our heavy footsteps echo in the cavernous space.

"Are you going to tell me what happened?"

I stop and turn back to him. "You don't want to wait for the rest of the guys?"

He shakes his head. "Preacher is ten hours into a massive hack, E has been holed up in his room, doing only God knows what for hours, and Rion made a grocery store run."

I snort and cross my arms over my chest. "Again? What does she need this time?"

Watching Rion turn into a sappy lapdog as soon as he found out Grace was pregnant has been quite entertaining. The man is as hard and cold as a fucking rock until that tiny redhead wants something. Then, he might as well be the father with the way he scrambles to make sure she's taken care of. Warwick appreciates it, but seeing Rion lose his edge over a woman who brought all sorts of trouble down on us irritates the fuck out of me.

The more you're willing to give, the more someone is going to take. It becomes nothing more than host and parasite with someone sucking the life out of you until you have nothing left, then leaving you to die.

Warwick glares and crosses his arms over his chest. "Are you ever going to stop this shit attitude?"

I continue to the table in the center of the vast room. We can have this argument a hundred times—we have—and it's not going to change how I feel about the Grace situation. Nothing will. "Unlikely, and we have more important things to worry about like the fact that someone else might've just taken out *Il Padrone*."

His dark eyes widen, and he clenches his jaw, the vein on the side of his neck bulging and throbbing with his anger. "What?"

I know how you feel, man.

We've all been looking forward to the day we could eliminate the Marconis. Someone else got to have all the fun.

I nod and drop into one of the chairs at the table. "Yep."

"What do you mean? What happened?" Heavy steps bring him to the table. He places his palms on the top and leans over it toward me.

I sigh, set the leash on the table, pull off my glasses, and rub my eyes. "I was watching them. A black SUV came around the corner, and it was like being back in fucking Iraq. Bullets were flying. Sounded like they were using AKs. *Il Padrone*, four of his capos, and one guard were taken down. I got out of there fast, so I didn't see if any of them survived."

"Holy shit. Did you see the shooter or get a license plate?"

I shake my head and shove my glasses back in place. "No. Windows were heavily tinted, and they were shooting from the other side. They were smart enough to take off the plate."

"Fuck." War steps back from the table and shoves a hand through his hair. "Who do you think is behind it?"

"Well," I lean forward and rest my forearms on the table, "that's the interesting thing. Arturo was eating lunch with them, and he got up and said something to *Il Padrone* before he disappeared inside the restaurant only a minute or two before the attack."

Warwick scowls and slams his fist on the massive piece of furniture. "That motherfucker. He isn't even trying to hide it, is he?"

"Could just be a coincidence. A random timing that played in his favor."

He scoffs and shakes his head. "No one's that lucky."

"Maybe. Maybe not. But it does beg the question...if *Il Padrone* is dead and Arturo did it, is the crew gonna let him take over?" Loyalties are always tested in situations like this. With *Il Padrone* dead, will they fall in line behind Arturo, regardless of whether they suspect he perpetrated the hit, or, will they revolt against him due to their loyalty to *Il Padrone*? "I sure as fuck hope not. The only thing worse than *Il Padrone* is Arturo."

War nods. "I agree. So, what do we do now?"

The door to the warehouse opens, and Rion storms in with three plastic grocery bags hanging off his arms. He eyes us. "What's going on? You figure out how to take out those assholes?"

I shake my head as he makes his way toward us. "Things got a little...complicated."

He drops the bags in front of his usual seat. "Like we don't have enough of that around here. What happened?"

Warwick heaves out a huge sigh. "Let's go get the rest of the guys so Cutter doesn't have to tell the story four times."

I grunt a thanks, and he pushes off the table and disappears down the hallway toward Preacher's nerd lair and E's room.

Rion narrows his eyes at me. "I don't like that look on your face."

"I don't like how your face looks ever, but you don't see me complaining."

He barks out a laugh and grabs the bags. "I'm taking these to the kitchen. I'll be right back to hear all the details of whatever clusterfuck you've gotten us into."

"Not my doing, though that doesn't make it any better."

"Christ, it's always something." He wanders behind me, off toward the kitchen.

He's right, though. Lately, it feels like we're constantly waiting for the other shoe to drop. Then a whole other set fall. It's a goddamn Lord of the fucking Dance around here with shit.

Is it really so much to ask for one *damn thing to go right?*

Warwick reappears with E behind him. Preacher brings up the rear, rubbing his eyes. I don't know how he spends so much time back there, staring at those screens without going blind.

They drop into seats around the table, and Rion returns with a beer in hand and pulls out the one next to me. He elbows me and taps his finger against his beer bottle. "So?"

I lean forward and rest my forearms on the wood. "So, *Il Padrone* and his capos were shot right in front of me."

"What?" E, Preacher, and Rion all ask in unison. The shock on their faces probably mirrors what I looked like when that SUV sped away.

"Yeah. No idea who did it, and our friend Arturo got up and left the patio right before it happened. The mystery woman who was with *Il Padrone* when he released Warwick and Grace was there, too."

Warwick narrows his eyes. "What was she doing there?"

I rock back in my chair. "Seemed to be guarding the big guy, but she left her post right before the shots were fired."

He scratches at his stubbled jaw and paces. "Suspicious."

"Definitely." I nod my agreement. "She and Arturo were the only two who walked away from that scene without at least one bullet in them."

Rion leans back in his chair and takes a swig of his beer. "Jesus, that really puts a damper on our plans, doesn't it? Is *Il Padrone* dead?"

"I doubt anyone could have survived that storm of bullets, but I don't have confirmation. I disappeared before the cops got there."

Preacher looks from me to Warwick. "What does this mean going forward?"

Warwick shrugs. "I don't know—" The satellite phone sitting in the center of our merry little group rings, and Warwick rolls his eyes. "Two guesses who that is."

Arturo.

He's the only one who ever calls us on it. The ringing is always a harbinger of bad news.

I nod toward it. "Well, answer it."

There's no sense in wasting time guessing about the fallout of the attack. We can get answers right here and now from the man who has always wanted *Il Padrone's* seat.

Warwick snatches the phone. His dark eyes move from me to all the other guys before he answers. "Hello?"

He presses a button to put it on speaker and sets it back in the center of the table.

"Mr. Pike." The familiar, hard voice of Arturo Marconi cuts through the line.

War wanders around to his usual chair and takes a seat. "Arturo, good to hear from you."

"Always nice to chat with you, too, Mr. Pike. How is everyone there?"

As if he actually gives a fuck...

The only thing Arturo cares about is Arturo.

"We are well. How are you?" Warwick asks his question through gritted teeth. Pleasantries with this man are difficult on the easiest of days. After what we know happened, pretending to keep things casual is a lesson in restraint.

"Well, I have some bad news, Mr. Pike. My uncle was gunned down today."

"What? That's awful..." War rolls his eyes. "Did they catch whoever did it?"

I chuckle at War's feigned distress over the shooting. If it were a week from now, I would have been taking *Il Padrone* and Arturo out in that exact same spot, and we'd be celebrating.

A momentary silence lingers on the line before Arturo clears his throat, feigning an emotional choke-up that we all know is as fake as his smile. "Unfortunately, not. It was a dark SUV with no plates. No other leads."

Warwick sucks in a breath and meets my gaze with a look that tells me I better keep my mouth shut. We have to play this stupid game with Arturo. It requires diplomacy I lack, which is why Warwick does all the talking on these calls. I wouldn't play these games with the man. I would call him out on his bullshit right from the start, but that's why Warwick leads us, not me. "Did he make it?"

Arturo releases a feigned sigh. "I'm sorry to tell you that my uncle is dead."

I clench my jaw and flex my hands. It's not that I hadn't

anticipated this. Like I told the guys, that patio was a damn slaughterhouse no one could walk away from, but that was *my* hit. My job. My chance to finally do something about our situation. Whoever those fuckers in the dark SUV were, they took away my chance to end this.

War swallows thickly. Time to lay on all that charm his mom taught him. "I'm so sorry for your loss."

Yeah, right. Sorry it wasn't us who did it and that Arturo didn't go to the grave with Il Padrone.

The line crackles before Arturo returns. "I appreciate that, Mr. Pike. It's a very sad time, but we need to talk about what this means for the organization and our agreement."

Warwick's dark eyes meet mine. "My agreement was with *Il Padrone*, not with you. I understand you will be inheriting the debt, but I expect you to abide by the terms of my original deal."

Arturo chuckles darkly in a way that says *you fucking moron; you would think that.* "I assume you have me on speakerphone with your crew."

"Yes."

"Well, gentleman, as you're now aware, my uncle is dead, which has left me in the position to take control of the family business. And I have a job for you."

I flex my hands on the table.

Warwick shifts uncomfortably in his seat. "Will you honor our agreement with *Il Padrone* that once the debt is paid off, we're free?" He clenches his fists in front of his chest as we wait for an answer.

He needs this. We all do. We all need to be free of the noose the Marconis have around our necks, but Warwick in particular. The surprise news of Grace's pregnancy has left him reeling. He's going to be a father and doesn't want to bring a child into this world, which is completely understandable. I'm an adult and a trained killer, and even I don't want to be working for the scumbag. But it's the only way to stay alive right now, so we'll continue to do what needs to get done until we find a way out.

Arturo chuckles again. "Straight to the point. Well, the specifics of our agreement can be discussed later. Right now, I have a job that is somewhat urgent."

Discussed later.

What he actually means is, he'll tell us how he plans to fuck us in the ass with a cactus later.

Warwick clenches his jaw. "What kind of job?"

The last *job* Arturo sent us on resulted in War taking Grace hostage, him almost dying after getting stabbed, and them being held for two days by Arturo when we couldn't replace the missing heroin. It doesn't exactly have us jumping to take another order from him.

"There's a cargo vessel leaving Sault Ste. Marie on Tuesday morning. I need you to intercept it along the way on Wednesday and take some cargo from the ship that belongs to me."

I snort and lean toward the phone. "If it belongs to you, why are we taking it off the ship?"

It's like he thinks we're fucking idiots. Warwick glares at me from the other side of the massive piece of wood. If he were closer, his hands would probably be around my neck. I probably shouldn't have chimed in, but the guy is seriously starting to piss me off. We aren't fucking stupid. We know what's going on. He's stealing from someone, more than likely a cartel because he doesn't have his own supply line.

A dark laugh comes from Arturo. "I don't know who just said that. Funny, though. Just get it done. I'll send you the details."

Warwick scrubs a hand over his face and sighs. "We'll keep you updated when we're on our way with the cargo."

"Wonderful. And Warwick?"

"Yes?"

"I look forward to a very lengthy working relationship." Arturo clicks off the line.

I grab the phone and power it down. The five of us around the table exchange looks. None of us expected to have to do another job for Arturo. He and *Il Padrone* should have been gone by this time next week. This is an unpleasant turn of events for everyone.

"I have a horrible feeling about this." Grace's soft voice floats over to us from where she stands at the base of the stairwell with her hand resting against her barely visible bump.

Warwick turns toward her. "Nothing to worry about, babe. It'll be fine."

She walks over and shakes her head. Her green eyes swim with worry. "I don't think so. I'm telling you...I have a bad feeling."

I hate to admit when Grace is right, but my Spidey senses have been tingling since the moment Arturo said he had a job for us. "I have a bad feeling, too, guys, but we still need to do the job. Arturo holds our nuts in a vise, for better or worse. It's not like we have any other option. If we say no, we die. At least if we have to say yes, we have a chance."

Rion frowns, downs the rest of his beer, and pulls a cigar from his pocket. He sticks it in his mouth but doesn't light it. He won't if Grace is in the room now. Another concession he's made to the woman who almost got us all killed, though there's no fucking way he will stop drinking. He chews on the end of it, the tension in his shoulders transferring to his jaw. The big man is just as pissed as I am about the current Arturo situation, but he has to know I'm right.

Preacher pulls out his phone and swipes at the screen a few times. "I got the info. Name of the vessel and schedule." He pushes away from the table. "I'm gonna go see what I can dig up on the ship and crew and start gathering what we need to lay out our plan of attack."

I rise to my feet. "That's what's most important here, guys, that we plan this. Every detail. We don't go in half-assed and ill-prepared." I look at Grace. "We all know what happened last time we went in thinking it would be a cakewalk. Look where that got us."

Warwick growls a low warning. "Watch it, man."

I hold up my hands and move around Rion's chair. "I just call it like I see it." I brush past Grace, and she reaches out to stop me, but I continue toward my room without a glance at her.

There's nothing to say. The way she came into this world, *our* world, the way she and Warwick ended up together, none of it sits well with me. She intended to betray us and fully admits it. Multiple times, she was poised to turn us over and do what was best for her even after telling us to our faces that we could trust her.

I would've done the same thing in her position, but when I'm the one on the receiving end of the selfish behavior, it doesn't exactly earn my confidence. There's no doubt she loves Warwick, but I don't believe she'll stay loyal if things ever go bad. Put that woman in an interrogation room, and she'd break. Quickly. I've seen it a thousand times. The ones with the strongest attitudes are often the easiest to crack, and that woman has attitude in spades.

Soft, late-afternoon light spills out of the half-open door to my room. I throw it open and find Milo snoring softly on the low bed in the center of the room. He's got the right idea. Food, minimal exercise, all the affection he could ever want from Grace and the five of us—the dog is living the good life.

I wander over and drop onto the mattress next to him.

When will we have that? When will we ever stop looking over our shoulders and watching our backs? When will the killing and violence stop?

Probably never, but I guess I signed up for this, quite literally.

I owe it to Warwick. If it weren't for him, I wouldn't even

be alive right now. Sometimes loyalty means putting your life on the line; other times, it means taking lives.

This requires both.

If I don't take out Arturo, our necks will forever be in the guillotine.

FOUR

Valentina

I *can't believe he even let me walk out of there.*
Arturo may not have wanted to shed blood in *Il Padrone*'s house, or maybe he wanted to do the dirty work somewhere private where he could confront me without an audience. That man is ruthless, and if he really knows why I'm here, he won't hesitate to take me out. So maybe I read too much into his words. Either way, I'm not taking any chances.

I can't go back to *Il Padrone*'s to get my things from my room. And I have to ditch the guy Arturo has following me. He isn't doing a very good job of concealing himself. None of these guys ever do. They're goons, plain and simple. Big bodies with no real skill or training. Not like me. The police force might not have been welcoming to a woman, but I didn't need them to be my friends to learn how to do my job well.

And my job now is finding proof that Arturo was behind the hit on *Il Padrone*. The first order of business is losing this guy.

The light at the corner in front of me turns yellow. There's plenty of room for me to stop, but instead, I check both directions and gun it through the intersection. My tail tries to swerve around the traffic. Horns blare, and tires squeal, but a quick glance in my rearview mirror assures me he's stopped at the light.

Sucker.

There's only one way I'm getting out of this alive, and that's by putting Arturo away, once and for all. If I can get enough to satisfy the police, Arturo will rot in prison for the rest of his life, and if it's not enough for the courts, the men who *were* loyal to *Il Padrone* will take care of him once they learn of the betrayal.

Either result is fine for me as long as he's gone.

The place to start is the restaurant and the man who was sitting across the street. He had to be involved somehow. Any innocent person would have stayed to assist in the investigation by describing what they saw.

I need to find him.

A light rain falls as I turn left and head back toward Moretti's. I glance down at myself and cringe.

I can't go around asking questions looking like this.

The gym clothes in the trunk will work. I pull up on a dark side street with little foot traffic, grab my bag, and climb in the backseat to change. The tank top, yoga pants, and tennis shoes are inconspicuous enough, but the blood still tinging my hands could be a problem.

I grab the bag of antibacterial wipes from my gym bag and scrub off as much of the staining as I can.

Don't think about what it is. Where it came from...

My eyes burn with unshed tears, and I blink them away and toss the wipes into my bag. A light pink still lingers in places, but I don't have time to spend trying to get my hands any cleaner.

Hopefully, anyone who sees me will think it's paint.

I can't do anything to draw attention to myself. Asking questions after something like this went down in the neighborhood will make everyone jumpy enough. If I'm going to get the answers I want, I have to be careful.

The lamp on the corner illuminates the street half a block from the restaurant. I make my way toward the patio that's still cordoned off with police tape. The crime scene techs scour the area, but I'm sure the most they'll be able to find are a few casings that may have fallen out of the window as the shooter sped away and potentially some tire tracks.

The guys who carried out the hit are professionals, and professionals know what they're doing. They don't make stupid mistakes.

And as much as I hate to admit it, Arturo's smart. He wouldn't use his own men. He would've hired somebody, and the man across the street was memorable. The sunglasses. The caramel-colored hair and facial scruff. And that dog. English Bulldogs are attention grabbers. Somebody had to have seen him.

Maybe someone knows him if he's been in the park before.

The area appears mostly deserted. It's too dark for the locals who may have been interested in the crime scene to see much. I pass the train station and make my way to the park.

Benches line the walking path, and I look over at Moretti's to make sure I'm at the right one. I lower myself onto the seat and stare across the street—the same view he had this afternoon.

But the park is deserted. There's not a single person out for an evening stroll or anyone walking their dog. Perhaps the shooting has made everyone stay in tonight. I can't say I blame them. Something that violent shakes you to the core. I know that all too well.

A car pulls into the train station parking lot, and its bright headlights shine in my eyes. I hold up my hand to block the light and glance down. Something glints in the lawn next to the bench. The car turns into a spot, but I keep staring into the thick, dark grass.

What was that?

I pull my phone from my pocket and turn on the flashlight as I slide down onto my knees. It's probably nothing. I'm not lucky enough to have something useful fall at my feet like this.

The light from my phone gleams off grey metal. I dig through the grass and come up with a bone-shaped tag. A dog tag. Hundreds of people walk dogs in this park daily, so what are the chances this has anything to do with the man who sat here today?

I hold it under the light. *"MILO"* is inscribed on one side. I turn it over. *"If found, call Cutter Jackson. (414) 555-0118."*

Cutter Jackson.

The name doesn't mean anything to me, but the tightness in my gut tells me this isn't random.

What are the chances this came from his dog?

There has to be a way to confirm it. Someone had to have seen something. I shove the tag into my pocket and make my way down the street where the man disappeared earlier.

Block after empty block, I make my way east. I reach an intersection with a stoplight, and a couple passes me, heading north. They enter a small shop with a glowing bakery sign hanging outside. The very recognizable shape of a dog on the sign has my heart pumping harder.

Perfect.

He had to have parked somewhere, and if he's a good dog owner, this is exactly the type of place he might stop to get a treat for his four-legged friend.

I casually stroll down toward the store. A security camera angled toward the street catches my eye. If he drove and parked anywhere near here, I may be able to get a license plate. But first, I have to gain access to the video.

A young girl, maybe high school or college-age stands behind the counter talking with the couple who walked in before me.

She nods at me. "I'll be with you in just a moment."

"Take your time." I wander around the small shop, examining the canine-themed artwork on the walls.

The couple exits, leaving me alone with the girl.

"Can I help you find something?"

I plaster on my friendliest smile. "Maybe. I'm looking for some information."

Her brow furrows. "What kind of information?"

I make my way over to the counter and lean against it. "Well, I think my friend may have been in here earlier with his dog and bought some treats. I want to get some more, so I'm hoping you can tell me what he bought."

She grins at the thought of another sale. "Oh! I can certainly try."

"Great. He has a bulldog named Milo."

"Oh!" Her eyes widen. "I remember Milo. They were in earlier this afternoon. Super cute dog. So sweet."

Yes!

Cutter Jackson has to be the man in the aviators. How many bulldogs named Milo can there be in this area?

"Yes," I nod and smile back, "he really is. Which is why I want to get some more treats for him." I already have the information I need. "I'll take whatever he bought."

She nods and taps her finger to her chin. "Hmm, I think I remember what he got. I'll package them up for you!"

I scan the store again while she bends to grab the treats. I couldn't care less about what she put in that bag. I have a name: *Cutter Jackson.*

Now, all that's left is to find him and get some answers.

She pops back up with a bag and holds it out to me. "That will be seventy-five dollars."

Seventy-five dollars! For dog treats?

A small price to pay to track down the man who may have been involved in *Il Padrone's* death, though. Well worth every single cent.

C *utter fucking Jackson.*
The man is practically a ghost.

After a quick stop at a store to grab a couple of bags of things, I've spent hours sitting at this crappy table in this mediocre hotel, poring over everything I could find online using his name and phone number. And it's basically nothing.

Former military, which would make sense if he were involved in the hit, but other than that, very little information is available. At least, publicly.

He keeps a low profile. Other than an article about his military enlistment after high school in Wisconsin, there's nothing about him as an adult. Not even a car registered in his name.

The military connection may be the only way to find out anything about him.

It's a good thing I didn't burn any bridges when I left Napoli. I pull out the burner phone I purchased and dial the international number. After I got here, I realized using my phone was probably as bad as being out in the open. Arturo has the kind of connections that make tracking a phone as easy as making one call.

"Hello?" Niall's smooth voice washes over me, the familiar British accent stirring something deep in me I thought long dead.

"Niall. It's Valentina."

"Val, love. How are you? Please tell me you're coming back."

I chuckle and shift in the shitty plastic chair. "Sorry, Niall, it's not in the plans right now."

Or anytime soon. When I left Italy, and all the people there, behind to help *Il Padrone*, I never anticipated I'd end up trying to find his killer. The plan *Il Padrone* put in place never had time to come to fruition. I may not be able to get it accomplished without him, but I damn well am going to try.

"If you're not coming back, to what do I owe this call?"

I suck in a deep breath and wince. "I need a favor."

One I hate asking for. I know what it means for Niall if he does it and gets caught, but there's nowhere else to turn, no one else I can turn to and trust.

"What kind of favor?"

"I need information on an American military man. He may be active or retired. I have a name and a phone number. I can't find much online."

Silence greets me from the other end as Niall considers my request. He clears his throat, and I can picture him leaning back in his chair with his booted feet up on his desk, a cold beer in his hand. "Who is this guy, love?"

I trust Niall, but I can't afford to trust anyone enough to tell them the full truth.

"Just someone I'm keeping an eye on."

Please don't press this further...

He releases a deep breath. "Let me see what I can do. Give me the name and number. I'll call you if I find anything."

"*Grazie.* Cutter Jackson. 414-555-0118. This is urgent, by the way. I will owe you big."

His deep chuckle practically vibrates through the phone, raising memories that make it even harder to know how long it will be before I see him again. "And how are you going to repay that if you're over there and I'm back here?"

A slow smile spreads across my face as I remember the last time I saw Niall. Two bottles of wine and a very naked night at his apartment. One of the many things I miss about Italy. "We'll figure something out."

"I'll get back to you." He hangs up, and I sit, staring at the computer screen again.

Had this happened back home, I would have a million

connections, countless ways to find other information, but here, I'm just a civilian foreigner on a work visa that's about to be terminated. *Il Padrone* got me here, but there's no way Arturo is going to do anything to help me stay.

Merda!

I run my hands back through my hair and tie it up with the band around my wrist. Sitting here, being completely useless with *Il Padrone's* death on my hands sucks. I can't do anything without more information. Which seems to be non-existent right now, and even if any of *Il Padrone's* men know anything, they'll be too terrified of Arturo to speak up. I just need to wait for Niall to hopefully get me what I need.

The shrill ring of the burner phone jerks me upright. I glance at the number. Niall.

That fast?

"Niall, you have something for me already?"

He lets out a deep sigh, one laced with annoyance and something else. "Why are you looking for this guy?"

"I already told you—"

"Don't lie to me, Val. This guy…You have no idea who you're dealing with."

Ice floods my veins, and I rise to my feet and eye my gun on the bedside table. "What do you mean?"

"What I mean is, imagine the most highly trained, lethal assassin on the planet, then multiply that by ten, and you get Cutter Jackson. You can't find anything about him because he doesn't want to be found. He's special ops. Probably Delta Force or some other secret division that does dirty work for the CIA. The best of the best. The guy is not going to let you find him if he doesn't want to be found."

"Does that mean you don't have an address?"

He scoffs and offers a mirthless laugh. "Of course, I have an address. Who do you think I am?"

It's exactly why I called him. His position in the SAS gives him access to the information and people to get it to him.

"Look, Val, I don't know how accurate this is, but his VA benefits are going to an address that comes up as a fishing company, of all things."

"A fishing company?"

"Yeah, a commercial fishing company. That's all I could find on him. Other than that, he doesn't exist. It's pretty clear; the guy's dangerous. Watch yourself."

The true concern lacing his voice tugs at my heart. I hated the way we left things. How *I* left. Quickly, without a real goodbye or any conversation about what we were to each other or where it was going.

"I always do."

Which is exactly why I need to find Cutter Jackson.

FIVE

Cutter

———————

The street in front of the Marconi family headquarters sits still and silent. Sporadic streetlights barely illuminate the front of the brick building purporting to be nothing more than the offices for the scrapyard behind it. No cars on the street or foot traffic at this time of night. And no movement in over two hours.

They chose this location well. It's far enough removed from the residential neighborhoods to produce few prying eyes or wandering neighbors. Plus, the noise from the car crushers and other machines in the yard that run during the day keeps people away. And this late, it's a practical ghost town around here.

Perfect for them. Boring as fuck for me.

This abandoned building across the street has been my home for the last week while I watch them. It's starting to become my least favorite place on Earth. The twelve hours I've sat here tonight have proved fruitless.

No sign of Arturo or the mystery woman—the only two people who know the truth of what happened yesterday.

Either he's chosen a new headquarters, or he's spending Saturday night celebrating his recently acquired position instead of hard at work on his new empire. A few of his men have come and gone, but there hasn't been any visible movement in so long, my damn ass is falling asleep.

I stand to get the blood circulating and remove the NODS goggles from my face. The tech that allows both night and thermal vision on these things is incredible and helpful, but fuck, even with them, the strain on my eyes becomes unbearable. I rub at them, then shove the amazing technology back into place over my eyes. It's the best way to see what's happening across the street. If either of them shows, I'm not letting them get away.

Though, it's looking more and more like that's not going to happen. Just like there's been no sign of Arturo, and whoever the mystery woman is, she sure as hell isn't here.

If she's Arturo's girlfriend, there's a chance she's at the estate, maybe even with him. If she were a plant—someone put in place to get close to *Il Padrone* to spy on him and find an opening—he may have paid her, and she may have already moved on. It would certainly be smart to get the hell out of Chicago before there's any chance of this coming back on her from anyone loyal to the old man.

Too many possibilities and unanswered questions for my liking. It's impossible to formulate a plan of attack when I have no fucking idea what's going on. All we have right now is speculation and supposition, and making any assumptions without cold, hard facts is what gets people in trouble. We've already had enough trouble to last us a lifetime.

This is a pointless waste of my time. I'm not going to get any answers.

Arturo isn't coming, and neither is she. It would have been nice to get my hands on her tonight. She's the only one who might be able to tell us who executed the hit and confirm it was at Arturo's order. The douchebag won't admit it to us himself. We need to know who all the players are before we can move another step toward taking out the new head of the Marconi family. Going in half-cocked doesn't do anyone any good and will only lead to more complications. Knowing who to trust in this game can mean life or death.

There's got to be another way to find her, another place to look for information.

But Preacher didn't exactly feel confident he could find much of anything when I spoke with him earlier. Other than a physical description and the fact that she worked for *Il Padrone*, we have nothing.

Christ…

Even describing her to him had my cock stirring to life. That long, sleek black hair. Tall and lean. Tanned skin. Nice rack. That heated gaze she shot from across the street.

She's good at her job. Excellent, actually. Not just anyone would have noticed me in the park and considered me a potential threat. That's why her leaving her post niggles at the back of my brain.

Why abandon the man you're protecting unless you want him dead?

There's no way to know the truth without questioning her. If she *is* working with Arturo, she has resources. If she tells him I was there, and he figures out I'm connected with Warwick, there's no telling what kind of wrath might come down on us. Because there's only one reason I would have been there—to take them out. A direct threat against Arturo means signing our own death warrants.

I swore to protect Warwick. To help him in any way possible, without question or reservation. I owe him, and I'm not going to let him down now. I'm going to find the girl and get some fucking answers. And then, Arturo and anyone else who might be a threat to us are going into the ground just like *Il Padrone*.

Preacher might be pursuing every avenue he can to get information, but his tactics take time—time we *don't* have. Only four days from now, we need to do yet another job for

Arturo. That doesn't leave much time to get the lay of the land and figure out what we're walking into.

Just another raid? A potential trap?

The closer we move toward that day, the more my unease grows. Sitting here is a waste. It's time to get back to the guys and figure out another way to track her down.

A flash of movement along the fence next to the Marconi headquarters straightens my spine. I switch from night vision mode to thermal. "Well, well, well, what do we have here?"

The familiar yellows, greens, oranges, and reds of a human. The shape shifts from behind a dumpster and scurries toward the back of the building. Even through the goggles and thermal imaging, the female form is unmistakable.

What are you doing, little mouse?

There's only one way to find out.

I race down the back stairs and out to the alley she snuck down. The silent street greets me, and I dart across it in the direction she moved. She had to be going in, but she definitely wasn't using the front door.

Why not?

Unease creeps up my spine as I peek around the back of the corner to the rear, where it faces the scrapyard. This could be a set-up. If someone spotted me, she could be leading me into a trap. Arturo may have baited the hook with her, and now, he's reeling me in.

I pause and scan the smooth brick of the building. A window halfway down stands partially open. That must have been her point of entry.

If it's a trap, why the sneaking around? And why here?

An alarm cord dangles uselessly on the inside of the window frame. It is a set-up—one she set up for *herself.* The wire was cut from the inside. She must have done it earlier, knowing she would come back tonight.

Smart.

And the action only further muddies the waters of what

the fuck is happening with her. All this clandestine bullshit is *not* what I expected.

I grab the windowsill and pull myself up and over into a small, dark room. I pull my Glock and flip my goggles over to night vision to find a tampon machine on the wall.

It's the women's bathroom.

A smile tugs at my lips despite my best effort. This is the last place any of these guys would ever think to check for a problem, which is likely why no one ever noticed the severed alarm wire.

Also smart.

The woman is more and more impressive, and she's far more than merely a bodyguard. It only adds to my belief that she's involved in the *Il Padrone* situation.

Maybe an assassin? Maybe a spy? Maybe both?

I inch open the door and listen. Silence. Not a whisper of noise or activity.

Where is everybody?

There should be at least two men still left in the building given who I saw coming and going today. They wouldn't leave this place unattended. Not with what goes down here. But now, there's no sign of them.

I ease from the bathroom and into the darkened hallway. A faint light slips from under a closed door across and to my left. It disappears then reappears. A moving flashlight? Someone is in there.

The girl? One of Arturo's men?

Either way, I need to know what's going on in there. I creep down toward the mystery light, but it vanishes. No sounds emanate from the room. I press my ear against the wood, but it doesn't help. I can't make out anything.

Dammit.

Mumbled voices from toward the front of the building jerk me back.

Shit.

I try the handle of the door across the hallway and duck into a storage closet. I'll take them out if I have to, but it would be better if no one ever knew I was here, especially the new head honcho.

Footsteps approach my hiding place. I tighten my hand around the gun grip.

A deep voice cuts through the solid wood between us. "I don't know. He just said to stay here tonight. He said he had a feeling something was going to go down."

Someone sighs. "I don't know why two of us need to stay. You really think she's dumb enough to show up here?"

"I don't know. She ditched her tail earlier, and she hasn't been back to her place. But I don't think she's gonna show. She'd have to be a fucking idiot. For her sake, I hope she went back to Italy."

Or really determined.

It sure as hell sounds like she's a target, not a member of the inner circle. But one thing I learned long ago, is that things aren't always what they seem. This doesn't mean she wasn't involved in a conspiracy to take out *Il Padrone.* Arturo may be after her now to eliminate anyone who can implicate him in the plot. She may be nothing more than a loose end. I won't make the mistake of underestimating her or giving her my back because I don't consider her a risk.

She's the worst kind of risk—an unknown one.

The voices and footsteps of the two men fade as they move away. Nothing but silence lingers outside the closet. I wait another minute to be certain before turning the handle and checking out what's happening.

Familiar eyes the color of amber meet mine through the cracked door across the hall—the one where I saw the faint light only moments ago. Long, thick black lashes frame them, and they widen. The woman raises her finger in front of her perfect, pink bow-shaped lips in the universal sign to be silent.

Dark hair sways around her face as she slips out into the

hallway while scanning it for Arturo's men. She slowly pulls the door closed silently behind her and then darts toward the back of the building, away from the direction the men headed.

Oh, no you don't. No way you're getting away from me, little mouse.

She may be the only one with the answers we need, and I'm not letting her disappear without getting them.

I slip out of the closet and close the door behind me, leaving no evidence I was ever here. There's no way to know what she was doing in the room across from me, but hopefully, she was smart enough not to leave any sign of her intrusion behind, either.

My footsteps don't make a sound as I follow the path she took toward the rear of the building. She stands in front of the back exit staring at it, and she mutters something under her breath. At my approach, she whips around and points a gun straight at my chest, mirroring my Glock pointed at hers.

"You. What the hell are you doing here?" Her heavily accented words are barely above a whisper, and her eyes dart down to the barrel of my gun before moving up to my face.

I sneer at her. "I could ask you the same thing."

And why the hell is she just standing here? Does she want to get fucking caught?

She scowls and glances over her shoulder toward our real only avenue of escape. "*Cretino.*"

SIX

Valentina

This idiot is going to get me killed. Leo and Eddie are just down the hall, their voices getting louder every second we stand here, and he wants to have a chat?

Cretino.

Footsteps echo toward us. The very real sound of doom approaching. They won't give us time to explain or let us escape. Shoot first, ask later. It's the motto of all of Arturo's men. We need to get out of here—*pronto.*

The man who seems intent on getting us killed glances at the door and then at me. "What's the problem? Let's go."

I shake my head, my gun still raised at him. I'm not letting down my guard around this man, not when he's as deadly as Niall seems to think he is. If he's here, it isn't with good intentions. "Are those goggles you're wearing blinding you?" I point at the door. "It's rigged with an alarm. I only cut the one on the window in the bathroom."

Because I wasn't thinking ahead. I snipped it two weeks ago, just in case I ever needed to get in without alerting anyone. I figured I would sneak out the same way tonight after I found evidence of what Arturo's been up to. My next stop tomorrow was going to be the fishing company Cutter has his check sent to, but it looks like I won't have to go searching for him anymore.

The cretino came to me.

He shoves me aside and slams his shoulder into the door and his body against the sign that clearly warns of the alarm. It bursts open to the alley alongside the building, and the shrill ring of the security system fills the hallway.

"Why the hell did you do that?"

He's just alerted the two *stronzos* back there that we're here. So much for getting in and out without anyone knowing. He shrugs. "No other way out. They would have found us anyway."

His rough hand grabs mine, and he tugs me through the door. Loud shouts and heavy footsteps thunder down the hall toward us.

He glances back toward the open door. "We gotta get out of here."

Oh, davvero?

The man who may very well be responsible for *Il Padrone's* death drags me down the alley toward the street. I pull on his arm and plant my feet. He tries to tug me forward, but I shake my hand loose. "Stop! My car is that way."

I point toward the rear of the scrapyard, the opposite direction we're heading.

He glowers and points forward. "Mine is that direction, and you're coming with me."

Who the hell does this guy think he is?

I'm not going anywhere with him. I may have wanted to find him, but I'm not stupid enough to jump into a car with him while he's armed and angry. No way. I turn to head toward my car, and a sharp pain slices at my arm as the crack of gunfire reverberates off the brick wall of the alley.

A volley of shots ring out, and Cutter returns fire, grabs me, and dives behind a large dumpster.

Merda!

Blood seeps through my long-sleeve shirt where the bullet hit my bicep. I clutch my arm and examine it in the dim light. "It's okay. It's just a graze."

Bullets ping against the dumpster. I peek around the side and return fire at Leo and Eddie. Hopefully, it's too dark for them to have gotten a good look at me. If Arturo knows I was here, he'll probably put a price on my head.

More bullets fly at me, and I duck back behind the protection of the metal monstrosity. I glance over at Cutter. Dark blood trickles out between his fingers where his left hand presses against a wound in his right shoulder.

He's hit.

I don't know what this guy has to do with Arturo, but I can't leave him here to die at the hands of these guys. I need answers and proof if I'm going to take Arturo down. Even if that means helping my enemy. I extend a hand toward him.

He pushes me away and points to a hole in the fence behind us. "That's our only way out."

A momentary pause in the gunfire leaves an eerie silence in the air. They must be reloading. We only have a few seconds.

He shakes his head, sets his jaw, rises to his feet, and bolts toward the fence. He pushes the opening wider with both hands, and I wince.

That had to hurt.

But it doesn't seem to faze him. He slips through the hole and takes off running without a glance back at me.

With a wound like that, most people wouldn't even be walking, let alone running. He's some sort of superhuman machine, or he's one of those freaks of nature who can't feel pain.

I climb through the hole in the fence and chase after him, down across the small side street and behind another building. Bullets whizz past us left and right.

Thank God Leo and Eddie aren't good shots.

If it had been any of Arturo's other men, we would be dead by now. These guys aren't exactly the top of the food chain for a reason. If the barrels of their guns aren't pressed against someone's head, they probably can't even perform a hit.

My feet pound on the pavement, and each gulp of air sends fire through my lungs. Keeping up with Cutter isn't easy. He darts into the darkness alongside a dilapidated building, and we pop out on another quiet, deserted side street. A black SUV sits a few feet away.

He runs toward it, grabs the door handle, and yanks it open. His eyes meet mine over the door frame. "Get in."

His door slams shut just as I reach the front of the vehicle, and the engine roars to life.

It's probably a bad idea to jump into a car with a man who, only seconds ago, had a gun pointed at me, but I need answers, and Leo and Eddie's shouts coming around the side of the building leave no other options.

I race to the passenger side, tug open the door, and climb in. Gunfire shatters the rear window, and more bullets clank on the metal of the SUV. Cutter throws it into drive and tears away, the tires squealing. I glance out the empty space where the window used to be at Leo and Eddie standing in the middle of the street, their guns raised. I empty my magazine at them.

More shots ping off the SUV as we turn the corner and speed away into the night. I relax slightly and glance over at Cutter, illuminated by the faint dashboard light. He grits his teeth and presses his left hand against his shoulder.

I pull on my seatbelt while keeping an eye on him. "Are you all right?"

"I'm fine." The words are practically flung at me.

Like this is somehow my fault?

He was there, too. He was just as likely to get shot on his own as with me. And he was the one who triggered the alarm on the door. I could have figured out another way to get out without leaving evidence.

The bright lights of Chicago speed past us as we head north, away from the only city I've ever been to in this country, away from everything I own and any resources or contacts I have. Dread sits like cold lead in my stomach, and I shift to face him more fully. "Where are we going?"

A grunt slips from his lips. "Away from here."

Not an answer. "To where?"

He snarls and glances over at me. The strange goggles covering his face prevent me from seeing his eyes. "None of your business, little mouse."

Little mouse?

"Little mouse? What does that mean?"

He snorts and shakes his head. "You were sneaking around like a mouse back there."

That's true. But referring to me as a rodent doesn't seem complimentary.

I set my spine and stare him down, even though his focus is on the road. "I have questions." Lots of them. Ones that I won't stop asking until I get answers.

He barks out a mirthless laugh and winces slightly, glancing down to where his bloody hand presses against his shoulder. "So do I, little mouse. So do I."

What could he possibly need to know?

He's not the one totally in the dark about what happened. He's not the one risking his life to get justice for *Il Padrone* and to prevent Arturo from hurting anyone else.

"Are you taking me to Arturo?"

Just because Leo and Eddie were shooting at him doesn't mean he's not on Arturo's payroll. He's got people everywhere —people from all walks of life. And Cutter's background is exactly what he looks for—a heartless military killer, someone who won't blink an eye at following through on a job, whatever is needed. Someone who won't have a conscience bothering them after they pull the trigger. So even if he wasn't the trigger man this time, at the very least, he could have been a lookout.

His head jerks toward me, and his lip curls. "What? Why the hell would I take you to Arturo?"

"Because he's your employer?" I cross my arms over my chest and wince at the pain in my arm. With all the adrenaline coursing through my system, I'd almost completely blocked out my injury. I glance down at it again. It's barely a flesh wound, and a few stitches will take care of it.

I can't say the same for Cutter's.

Blood soaks his shirt sleeve and covers the driver's seat beneath him. Drops fall onto the center console with a sickening *thump* every few seconds.

I keep my focus on him and only glance up at the road occasionally. We're well past the city now with the suburbs flying by us as we head north toward Wisconsin.

He doesn't give much away. And except for the occasional tic of his clenched jaw, I wouldn't even know he'd been shot and is bleeding to death. He doesn't respond to my accusation about being on Arturo's payroll. He doesn't acknowledge I even spoke.

Silent treatment it is, I guess.

But I can't let him die before I get my answers. "We need to get you to a hospital."

He grunts. "I'm fine. I've survived worse."

No doubt, he has. The occasional passing lights from the roadside buildings illuminate the pink and red scarring that climbs up his neck, disappears under his facial scruff, and then reappears along his cheek and up around his eye. The goggles he wears, that likely have night vision and some other tech to give him an advantage, hide a lot, but they can't hide that.

But no matter how tough someone is, we all bleed the same, and he's bleeding. *A lot.*

I shift in my seat to look out at a passing road sign that

announces we're about to cross into Wisconsin. "You won't tell me where we're going, but I hope it's close. You won't make it long bleeding like that."

He keeps his attention on the road, but his right hand tightens around the wheel, turning his knuckles white. He knows I'm right, and with his training, he's not dumb enough to let this continue much longer without treating himself.

The next exit appears, and he jerks the wheel and takes the ramp fast, the tires screeching. He pulls off onto the dark frontage road and stops on the gravel shoulder. My hand tightens on my gun where I have it at my hip, but it won't do me much good anyway. I'm out of ammo. He throws the SUV in park and turns to face me. "There's a bag in the trunk. Go get it."

"Excuse me?"

He sneers at me. "You heard me. Go get the bag and also grab the roll of duct tape from the toolbox while you're back there."

I glower at him. Macho guys like him tried to boss me around and give me shit every day on the force. I didn't let them get away with it, and I'm not about to let this guy do it. "What makes you think I want to help you?"

A low growl slips from his quivering lip as he leans over the center console toward me. He stops with his face mere inches from mine, the heat radiating off his body, permeating me even with the distance between us. "Because I just fucking saved your life."

I open my mouth to retort but almost immediately clamp it shut. Not because I don't want to argue.

He's right.

There's a chance I could have managed to get out through that bathroom window again or find another place to hide until I could get out another way, but it was unlikely given that Leo and Eddie were already on their way down the hall.

Enemy or not, Cutter took a bullet for me and pulled me out of the line of fire.

An infuriating smirk spreads across his lips. Cutter knows he has me on that, and something tells me, for as long as we're stuck together like this, he's not going to let me forget what he did for me. "Now, go get what I asked for."

This asshole ever heard of the word "please?"

I shove open the door and walk around to the trunk of the SUV. He presses something inside that pops open the door. A large duffel bag and a small toolbox sit in the otherwise empty space. I open the toolbox and grab the roll of duct tape before snagging the bag and slamming the door.

The man is maddening. He's bleeding to death, and he still has an attitude with me. The only reason I'm even helping him is that he *did* save my life back there. But I still don't trust him.

Patch him up. Find your answers. Get the hell away from him.

That's the plan...for now. I climb back into the SUV and set the bag on the floor at my feet.

He nods toward it. "There should be a clean shirt in there. Grab it."

"Didn't your mother ever teach you to say please? That asking nicely gets you further in life than making demands?" I rummage through the bag and find a white T-shirt under a pair of jeans. "You don't need to be a dick."

He snorts out a laugh. "I don't need to be a dick? Who the fuck do you think you are, *principessa?*"

I tear the T-shirt into strips with a little more aggression than is probably needed. "*Sei proprio un coglione. Ma che cazzo? Principessa?*"

"If the glass slipper fits, *principessa*. Before you insult people, you should make sure they don't understand Italian."

I freeze and squeeze my eyes shut.

He's understood everything I've said? Every name I called him? Merda.

I turn toward him with the ripped strips from the shirt. He removes his hand from the wound, and blood flows freely, thick and red, and drips against the console separating us.

My stomach clenches, but not from anger or distrust or because I'm squeamish at the sight of a gnarly wound and blood. No, it's because I've seen wounds like this before, and unless where Cutter's taking me is close, he's losing too much blood to make it. "That doesn't look very good."

His clenched jaw tics. "No shit, Sherlock."

These American expressions don't make much sense to me, but I get the reference and the sarcasm dripping from his words.

"You want help or not?" I raise an eyebrow.

He reaches for the strips of soft material on my lap, and I knock his hand away. Before he can react with another insult or jibe, I push one of the folded strips against the wound. Hard.

Another growl rumbles from his chest, and he struggles to hide his wince.

I grab his hand and replace mine with it. "Hold this."

He scowls but bites back any retort he was about to make while I unroll the duct tape. The tension in the front seat thickens as I wrap the tape around the wound. He doesn't utter a word or flinch, but the electricity arcing between us with every brush of skin has my blood heating. I press the tape together to seal the temporary bandage, maybe a little harder than I need to. Again, no reaction from him as he examines my handiwork.

The man is tough as nails; that much is evident. And considering the line of scars running up his neck and right cheek to disappear behind the side of the goggles, he's already seen some serious shit. I want to ask about what happened, but he won't answer anyway. There's only one reason someone wears glasses all the time, and it's not to cover something beautiful.

The silence is starting to get uncomfortable, and I shift back in my seat, putting some much-needed distance between us. "You have to get this taken care of. You're going to bleed to death. Even if it didn't hit an artery, it might have nicked something."

He shakes his head. "No hospitals. They're required to call the police right away when there's a gunshot wound."

Dannazione!

Of course…The same thing would happen in Italy. And if the cops arrive, we would have a lot of explaining to do and would likely both end up in custody. There, I won't be getting any answers.

I chew on my lip as I consider my options. There aren't many. Cutter needs treatment. Fast. "How much farther? Can you at least tell me that?"

"Another couple of hours." The unease in his voice is evident even to someone who barely knows him. He knows how bad it is, too.

"So, what are we going to do?"

He sighs and looks down at the bandage. "What we just did. Pack it, wrap it, and pray."

SEVEN

Cutter

———————

The wound is nothing.

Well, maybe not nothing, but nothing I can't handle.

I've had worse. I've had to dig myself out from under the bodies of my brothers, burned-out trucks, and debris. I've had to try to help save the lives of those who managed to survive the initial blast while almost a quarter of my body was covered in third-degree burns and riddled with shrapnel.

I survived that. I'll survive this.

If this woman doesn't drive me to my death first.

She has no business asking questions or giving me this attitude. I just saved her damn life. They were going to kill her. Or me. Both of us, probably. The least she could do is show a little fucking appreciation.

But a beautiful woman like her is probably used to batting her thick, dark lashes in a man's direction, pursing those perfectly plump lips, and getting whatever she wants. The way her slightly tan skin practically glows in the moonlight only emphasizes her beauty. That face could've been painted by Michelangelo himself.

Yeah, she's probably never heard the word "no" in her life.

Fucking princess.

She's spoiled and demanding, and she's the enemy right now and maybe forever—even if she makes my dick twitch. I'd reach down to adjust it, but I need a hand on the wheel, and holding my right arm up to drive with it isn't possible anymore.

The edges of my vision blur, and I squeeze my eyes shut and shake my head slightly to keep my focus on the highway in front of me. Our exit is next.

Thank fuck.

Maybe I underestimated how much blood I'm losing. The makeshift bandage *principessa* slapped on me was only a shoddy, temporary fix. Blood still trickles down onto the seat below me and has been for the uncomfortably silent two hours that have passed since I pulled off the highway to slap something on it.

At least a dozen times, the heat of her gaze lingering on me had my skin breaking out in goose bumps. Or maybe that was my body temperature dropping due to the blood loss. Either way, the feeling wasn't welcome.

I veer off the highway, down the exit ramp, and onto the small two-lane road that leads toward the warehouse. The pitch-black pavement before me grows even darker, as does the rest of the world in my peripheral vision.

A small hand squeezes my thigh. "Cutter? Are you all right?"

"I'm fine." I somehow manage to grit the words out through my clenched teeth but just barely.

Rion will get me stitched up good as new. Everything will be fine. Warwick and I will question her. We'll find out what we need to know. Then, we'll figure out what to do about *principessa.*

My turn onto the gravel road to the warehouse sends rocks flying out into the trees that line both sides.

Principessa shifts in her seat and stares out at the dark woods. "Where the hell are you taking me?"

The fear in her question makes her voice shake. I can't say I blame her. I'm driving her down a dark road with nothing around for miles. It's the perfect recipe for rape or a bloodbath.

Rape isn't our style, but I can't guarantee she'll walk away without bloodshed. Whatever it takes to get what we need.

Light finally filters through the trees ahead, and the warehouse comes into view. I slam on the brakes. The SUV screeches to a stop outside, and I throw it into park and turn it off. *Principessa* leans forward and stares up at the massive structure.

It doesn't look like much from out here, but we've managed to make it a home over the last five years. The dilapidated appearance of the exterior helps conceal us and all the tech Preacher's managed to acquire for us, like the camera above the warehouse entrance trained on us right now.

I force myself to suck in a deep breath and push open the door.

You can do it, Cutter. Just get in there. A dozen steps.

Gritting my teeth, I drop my feet onto the gravel and shove myself up. The world spins, and I grab the frame of the SUV to steady myself. I can't end up face-first in a pile of rocks in front of this woman.

The passenger door slams, and then, a small arm slides across my back and pulls me upright.

"No." I shove her away and take a wobbly step forward, my hand still braced for support. "I got this." Even if I can't stand on my own two feet, I'm not leaning on this woman. I've been through worse. I can get through this. Alone.

I stagger toward the warehouse.

Rion charges out, his hands fisted at his sides, his dark eyes blazing. "Where the hell have you been, man? We've been..." His gaze narrows on the duct tape bandage. "Jesus, what the fuck happened to you?" He glances toward the SUV where *principessa* still stands near where I just stumbled out. "Who the hell is she?"

Good fucking question.

I force a smile, one Rion is sure to recognize for what it is —a fucking cry for help.

He races forward and slips an arm around me. "Want to tell me who the fuck that is?"

"I don't have a name, but she's the one I told you about."

Rion peeks over his shoulder and flashes a taunting grin at her before turning back and helping me toward the safety of the warehouse. He winks at me. "I'm sure we'll get it out of her."

No doubt.

Just as soon as I'm cleaned up, we'll get down to business.

We pause so Rion can pull open the door, and I take the second to glance back. She approaches with concerned eyebrows dropped down low over her uncertain eyes and her bottom lip tucked between her teeth.

You should be worried, principessa.

"Preacher! E! Warwick!" Rion's voice booms through the open space, and he walks me toward the table in the center of the room.

But it's the tiny redhead who threw our world into chaos who appears at the entry to the kitchen, not one of the guys. "Oh, my God. What happened?" Her eyes hit my female companion, and they widen. "Warwick..." She looks over her shoulder into the kitchen.

War appears behind her, his coal-black eyes narrowed on our visitor and me. He leans forward to whisper something to Grace before he hands her a bowl and storms toward us with Milo at his feet.

Rion manages to wrangle me to the wood slab we always gather around. He helps me climb up and presses on my chest to get me to lie back.

Thank fuck.

I don't think I could've walked another six feet to my room or down to Rion's makeshift infirmary.

"Jesus, again?" Preacher appears at my side and stares down at me. "Didn't we learn anything from Warwick's little incident with the knife a few months ago? Avoid sharp objects and bullets being put into your flesh."

I sneer at him. "I'm fine."

He crosses his arms over his chest. "Yeah? You sure look fine." He glances over at the woman at the center of this shit. "Who is she?"

Warwick steps up next to Preacher and nods at our "guest." "She's the woman I told you guys about who was guarding *Il Padrone* when Grace and I were *guests* of Arturo."

I motion toward where she stands halfway between us and her means of exit. "She's also the one who rather conveniently abandoned him right before Arturo left the old man and everybody else was shot to fuck."

She glowers at me but doesn't say anything, merely crosses her arms over her chest and tries to look tough as she assesses each of us and then turns to evaluate the way we just came in. No doubt checking out avenues of escape.

Not while I'm still breathing. "You need to keep an eye on her."

Her anger darkens her cheeks, and she huffs but remains silent.

Probably smart considering she's outnumbered and outgunned and has no idea where we are.

Warwick nods at me. "So, what happened?"

"I caught her sneaking into Arturo's offices. The two goons he left to watch the place used us for target practice."

He runs a hand through his hair. "Well, shit. How badly were you hit?"

Rion reappears, pushing the giant cart of medical supplies that he's upgraded since Warwick's incident. "We'll find out right now." He grabs a giant pair of scissors, puts it to the hem of my shirt, and cuts upward. "Hope you don't have any senti-mental attachment to this shirt."

I snort as he pulls the shredded fabric from my body.

A tiny gasp floats from *principessa*.

My scars.

People are never ready for them. Even the nurses at the VA when they came in to treat me had trouble making eye contact or looking directly at them. I get it—they're ugly. The way they snake along my right side and up over my shoulder and neck onto my face can be stomach-churning.

Rion cuts the duct tape from around the wound. "This is gonna hurt."

No shit.

He presses against the wadded-up strips of T-shirt, then pulls them back slowly. I grit my teeth and clench my fists at my sides. Rion's bedside manner could use some improve-ment, but I respect the way he never coddles anyone, even in the worst of circumstances—and this is *far* from the worst he's seen.

The frown turning down Rion's lips needs no interpreta-tion. "Shit, man. This is bleeding pretty badly. It may have nicked something. But I don't really know if there's anything vital damaged. It will take a few minutes to dig around a little bit to see what's going on."

Fucking great.

He examines the wound and wipes away more blood oozing out. "How much blood did you lose getting here?"

"A lot." The answer comes from the woman who looks torn between bolting for the door and jumping in to help with the procedure. "Too much. I've seen enough gunshot wounds to know that's bad."

"Shit." Warwick twists back toward the kitchen, and I drop my head to the side and find Grace leaning against the doorjamb. "Grace, go grab the IV stand and the rest of the supplies from the infirmary."

She nods and disappears down the back hall. Elijah passes her on his way toward us. His focus narrows in on me, then darts to *principessa.*

I nod toward her. "This is gonna get messy. Get her out of here."

There's no way I'm letting this woman watch me get cut open. And we don't need to be watching our backs with her here.

E approaches the table and leans down to me. "What do you want me to do with her?"

"Lock her in the storeroom. And take her gun." She may be out of ammo, but that doesn't mean she's not dangerous with it.

He narrows his gaze on her. "Are you gonna cause any trouble?"

She pinches her lips together and shakes her head. "No, and I can help. I have some medical training."

Rion's head snaps up. "How much?"

She hesitates briefly. Answering will give us more information about her. She's smart enough not to want to offer anything. "Not a lot. A few incidents where I had to take charge of a scene until someone else got there."

A scene?

No one talks like that except a cop.

But what the fuck would a cop be doing working for Il Padrone?

Rion waves her over. "Better than nothing."

I grab his wrist. "What the fuck, Rion? You're going to let her help? We don't know who she is or what the hell she wants—"

He glares at me while he presses against the wound even harder than before.

I try, unsuccessfully, to pull away. "Fuck! What the hell was that for?"

"Do you want to die? If not, then I suggest we take all the help we can get."

Well, when he puts it like that.

I offer a grunt of agreement and turn my head as much as I can away from where she stands across from Rion.

Rion leans down to me. "I need to take off the NODS." His words are low and whispered, but in my peripheral vision, I catch her head jerk to look at us when he speaks.

I clench my fists. "Why?"

He scowls at me. "Because I need to be able to see your eyes to make sure you're under before I start this. I'm gonna have you hooked up to all sorts of stuff, but I also need the eyes. I'm sorry."

He knows what it means to be exposed like that, especially in front of her—someone we know almost nothing about except that she's probably bad news—but there's no choice. I nod, and he reaches out and pulls them off.

The bright overhead lights momentarily blind me, and I squeeze my eyes shut against it. There's no point in trying to hide it anymore, though. She's going to see one way or the other. I turn my face toward her and stare her down with my one good eye.

Her lips part, and an almost silent gasp slips between them before she catches herself and presses them firmly together. She winces and quickly averts her gaze, focusing on the medical supplies Rion is lining up along the table.

The scarring. The clouded, sightless, milky-white, mangled right eye.

It's something no one should ever have to see, yet I see it every time I look in a mirror, which is why I avoid them more than I did my parents as a teenager.

I turn my head back so I'm staring up into the bright overhead light. "Let's do this."

"Grace! Do you have the IV?" Warwick's voice booms through the massive space.

"Coming!" A moment later, she appears directly above the table and hands Rion several things before turning her attention to me. Her soft-green eyes meet mine, and her lips twist down with something I'm all too familiar with...

Pity.

In all the months Grace has been here at the warehouse, I've managed to keep it hidden from her, but now, it's out there. My biggest weakness. The thing that ripped me away from the only job and only life I ever knew. The damage that prevents me from doing what I'm exceptionally fucking good at—the fatal flaw to my career.

Warwick leans in and presses a kiss to her temple. "Go upstairs, please. You won't want to see this. Take Milo."

She opens her mouth to argue, but he gives her the look— the one we all know means not to fucking say another word. It's something Grace loves to rebel against, but tonight, she relents and scoops up Milo before she turns toward the stairway leading up to their bedroom without a word.

Good.

Grace and I may never be on good terms, but even if we were, I wouldn't want her to see this. If I had any option, I wouldn't let *anyone* see it.

Rion finishes lining up the items he needs along the top of the cart and table. He disappears with Preacher into the kitchen for a minute, probably to wash their hands before the procedure, and returns to lean over me. His worried gaze meets mine. "You ready for this, Cutter?"

"As ready as I'll ever be."

"Good, 'cause this is going to hurt."

EIGHT

Valentina

Hurt is an understatement. What this guy is about to do to Cutter is not something that should be attempted outside of the hospital and not unless under complete sedation. The fact they're doing this in a rundown warehouse speaks volumes about what kind of men they are. And now that I've seen Warwick, I know a hell of a lot more and better understand what's really going on.

Il Padrone explained his deal with Warwick and his crew to me months ago when Arturo had Warwick and Grace held at his estate. To say the old man wasn't happy with the situation would be putting it mildly. He was a hard man—a very hard man—but he was fair, and what Arturo was doing to them was anything but.

Cutter's part of Warwick's team which means they likely could be behind the assassination. They have every reason to want to take out *Il Padrone* and Arturo to get out from under their control. Neither one was going to let them off the hook until their debt was completely repaid.

Il Padrone may have let up on them once he'd received every cent he was owed, maybe come to a new agreement under which they continued to work together that was more favorable to Warwick's crew, but not Arturo. He knows when he has somebody by the balls, and he has all five of these guys.

The monstrous man Cutter called Rion—who's about to slice into Cutter—locks eyes with me as he pulls on surgical gloves. "Okay, you, what's your name?"

Do I give him my real one? At this point, what does it matter? They'll know soon enough anyway, right?

"Valentina."

Cutter doesn't move on the table. He doesn't even open his eyes. No reaction whatsoever to me finally giving my name. But he definitely heard it.

Light glints off a scalpel and some other procedure items as the big guy rearranges them on the tray. "Right, Valentina, you stay on that side. Preacher, assist me over here."

The tall guy with the short beard who must be Preacher moves from the foot of the table around to stand next to the big guy. Warwick leans over Cutter at the head of the table and taps him on the forehead. Cutter's eyes open, and he stares up at Warwick.

The corner of Warwick's lips tips up. "Don't die, fucker."

"I'll try not to." Cutter's eyes drift closed again, and he seems to relax, some of the earlier tension leaving his body on a long, slow exhale.

Warwick turns to Preacher and Rion. "Don't let him die."

They both chuckle, and Preacher pulls on latex gloves and hands me a pair. "I know Rion and I are invested in keeping him alive, but what about you?" His narrows his blue eyes on me.

I tug on the gloves and nod at Preacher and Rion. "If he dies, I don't get the answers I need." There's no need to tell them that if I find out they are behind *Il Padrone*'s death, I'll kill them all myself. "What do you need me to do?"

Rion nods toward the IV stand Grace brought from somewhere down the hall. "I want to put you in charge of watching his IV and checking his vitals."

Okay, easy enough.

I nod my agreement and watch him insert an IV into Cutter's left arm. Cutter doesn't move. He doesn't even acknowledge the needle penetrating his skin.

Preacher injects something into the IV line, probably some sort of anesthetic, and he slips what appears to be a pulse ox monitor onto Cutter's finger. Preacher wraps a blood pressure cuff around Cutter's arm, then glances up at me. "You, watch that, too."

"Got it." I nod again.

Rion pauses for a second and locks eyes with me. "I want you to take his blood pressure every five minutes. If the systolic drops below eighty, you let me know. If his heart rate goes over one-forty or drops below fifty, you tell me immediately. Also, watch his blood ox. Less than ninety-four percent, I need to know. I'm also going to need you to watch his breathing. Place your hand on his chest, nipple high. Less than eight a minute, we're in trouble. Just keep me updated."

It's a lot of information to process, a lot to keep track of, but I can do it. "Okay."

He grabs a scalpel. "Let's do this."

Cutter's eyes fly open. The milky film covering his right eye and the ugly scarring that covers that half of his face certainly explains the goggles never coming off during that drive. For a man like him, it's a physical weakness, and these types of men never show any chink in their armor. Given the state of his whole right side, it's pretty obvious, this is why he left the military.

Something horrific happened to him that left him like this and maybe gave him his shitty attitude, too.

Though maybe he was just born with that…

Rion stares down at his friend, and something serious passes between them. "I got you, man."

With a little nod, Cutter closes his eyes again without a glance or acknowledgment in my direction.

The "surgeon" places the scalpel over the bullet wound. "Cutter? You still with us?"

Cutter mumbles something incomprehensible but doesn't move or open his eyes. Whatever they put into his IV has taken effect.

"Cutter?" There's no response at all this time. Rion leans over him and lifts the lid on Cutter's left eye. He glances up at me. "He's out. Here we go."

The scalpel slices through the skin around the wound, and more blood wells and drips down Cutter's scarred body. Rion narrows his eyes and probes around the damaged area.

I check all of Cutter's vitals and suck in a shaky breath. Everything seems okay so far, but that doesn't mean much. Who knows how long this might take or when things might go south fast?

Rion glances back at Preacher. "Shit. It nicked the subclavian vein. No wonder he was bleeding so badly." His dark eyes flick up to meet mine. "It's been bleeding like this for three hours?"

"At least that long. We wrapped it and slowed it down somewhat."

"Shit. Shit. Shit. Shit. He needs a blood transfusion. He's lost way too much. If we don't get some more blood volume into him, he's going to crash."

I saw it coming, but the words still send a cold chill down my spine. "A blood transfusion? We have to go to the hospital."

Warwick smacks his palm against the foot of the table. "No hospitals. Can you do it here, Rion?"

Rion turns to make eye contact with Warwick. "I mean, I can, but I don't know everyone's blood types."

I grit my teeth and shake my head as I let out a mirthless laugh. This entire situation has become one giant joke...*on me*. "I'm O-negative."

Rion's jaw drops. "You're shitting me."

I shake my head again. "Nope. I'm O-negative."

Warwick throws up his hands. "What does that mean?"

Preacher points at me, relief written all over his bearded face. "It means she's a universal donor. It means her blood will work with anyone."

One of Warwick's dark eyebrows wings up. "So...we're good?"

Rion's eyes search mine. "We're good if she's willing."

I stare down at the one person who potentially holds the answers I need—his pale, clammy skin and weakening vitals.

A swirl of script under his left rib cage reads *"Illegitimi non carborundum."*

Don't let the bastards grind you down.

It's a fitting mantra for a man with a background like Cutter's. He survived something horrible. And he did save my life. I would never have been able to get back to my vehicle from there—Leo and Eddie were blocking my only avenue of escape—and he knocked me down behind that dumpster and took that bullet doing so. I owe him.

Maybe God will smile down upon me if I do this good deed.

A shaky breath slips from my lips. "Let's do it."

It's just a little blood. I've donated dozens of times over the years. This is no different. It's simply going directly into someone instead of into a plastic bag.

Rion nods and looks to Warwick. "Grab one of the transfusion kits. Then, we need to lay her down next to him. I'm done here and can get him stitched up while you're working on that."

Warwick digs through the cart of medical supplies while Preacher hands Rion everything he needs to suture the wound. Silence fills the huge warehouse as Rion meticulously closes Cutter.

For such a huge man with such massive hands, Rion sure knows how to do delicate work. He ties off the sutures and sighs as he rises to his full height. "I sure hope I got all the bleeders."

Preacher nods down to Cutter. "You're too good to fuck up, and he's a fighter. You know what he's already survived. This is nothing. This isn't the way he goes out."

"I hope not." The concerned bunch of Rion's brow tells me he's not so sure. "Let's just get this transfusion done and pray."

Pray?

These guys don't seem the praying type. In fact, I figured the nickname Preacher came from something else, but he leans over Cutter, slips out a chain around his neck to grasp the cross hanging from it in his hand. *"Ángele Dei, qui custos es mei, me, tibi commíssum pietáte supérna, illúmina, custódi, rege et gubérna.* Amen."

Profound words, and in Latin nonetheless, for a man who's a pirate. But something tells me, there's a lot more to these guys than meets the eye, especially the man on the table before me.

I pray he lives long enough for me to figure out what it is and what his role in everything has been.

He's an enemy until proven otherwise.

"Trust no one." It's one of the first things *Il Padrone* told me when I landed in the States.

He didn't trust Arturo, his own nephew; there's no way I'm going to trust this guy. Arturo underestimates me and the lengths I'm willing to go to uncover the truth and make him pay for what he did.

It would be easier if I had help, but I'm more than capable and willing to do it alone. I've always been alone, and if I have to take down Arturo Marconi by myself, I will.

NINE

Cutter

S omething breaks through the black cloud enveloping me.
Something sharp.

Something burning.

Pain.

My old friend.

I grit my teeth against fire in my arm and force open my heavy lids. Dim early morning light pours in through the open window of my room along with the familiar scent of Lake Michigan and the cries of the seagulls that circle the lighthouse down the beach.

Why the hell aren't the curtains pulled?

I reach out for Milo, but all my palm finds is the soft, crisp sheets. He's not in his usual spot along my left leg. There's no way that dog would leave me voluntarily. The guys must be keeping him away. Little guy won't be thrilled about that. He's been my constant shadow since Warwick brought him to me as a tiny puppy in the hospital all those years ago. Not waking up with him snoring lightly beside me has my chest aching almost as much as where Rion cut into me.

Almost.

I shift to try to push myself up with my left hand, and pain

73

slices through my arm and into my chest. Deep breaths are the only thing that prevents me from yacking all over my bedroom floor. Whatever they gave me as anesthesia isn't sitting well this morning. Add in pain, and it's a bad mix. Almost as bad as my twenty-first and all those Jagerbombs. To this day, even the smell of Red Bull makes me want to puke.

Fucking A.

My bedroom door shoves open, and a column of artificial, fluorescent light shines in and lands on my bed. I blink against it and hold up my left hand to cover my eyes.

"I thought I heard you moving around in here." Rion steps into the room, his massive frame blocking out the offending light, and I drop my hand and lie back on the bed. "How you feeling?"

I manage a chuckle that sends pain radiating through me again. "Like I got shot."

At least it was in the arm. There are a lot of worse places to take a bullet. I've seen those results and wouldn't want to live them personally.

Rion moves over next to the bed and squats. "You were in pretty bad shape. Had to give you a transfusion."

"What?" I must have misheard him. The lingering drugs in my system must be fucking with my hearing. Because doing a transfusion here would be crazy and impossible given blood-typing issues.

"A transfusion."

I guess my brain wasn't playing tricks on me. "How the hell did you manage that?"

Amusement plays in his dark eyes, and he nods toward the main warehouse. "Turns out that mystery woman you brought back here, Valentina, is O-negative."

Motherfucker.

"Valentina? That's her name?"

He nods. "She told us last night right before the procedure. You don't remember?"

A fuzzy memory of the hard table at my back and murmured voices surfaces. "Vaguely, I guess. And she agreed to be a human blood bank, just like that?"

He shoves a hand back through his hair. "Surprised the hell out of me, too, but it worked. Your blood pressure is good. Your temp is good. Everything looks fine." He nods down toward my shoulder. "As long as we can keep that from getting infected." He rises and walks around to a hanging IV bag. "I've had antibiotics going while you've been out."

"Thanks, man."

He shakes his head with a smirk. "Don't thank me. Thank Valentina. I don't think you would've made it without the transfusion."

Well, shit.

Being indebted to the woman who could be behind Arturo's rise to power is not a position I want to be in. "Where is she?"

Rion tips his head back toward the warehouse. "Preacher is trying to dig up some more information on her now that we have a first name, but she's not saying much."

I try to push myself up again but end up dropping back down onto the bed to avoid another fight with nausea. "You assholes better not be trying to interrogate her without me. You tell Warwick to leave her the fuck alone. She's mine."

Rion holds up his hands and shakes his head. "No interrogation. Just a few basic questions, but we can't hold out much longer. We have to be on that ship in three days, and we know nothing about her or why she's involved in this situation."

"Exactly my point. We need to be careful."

He nods his agreement. "Very."

"Where's Milo?"

He barks out a laugh. "We sent him off with Grace to keep him from climbing all over you while you were out. That damn dog is worried about you more than I can explain."

I'm not surprised. I have yet to meet anyone as loyal as

that dog, though, Warwick, Preacher, E, and Rion do come damn close. I struggle to raise myself onto my elbow, but I only end up wincing and gritting my teeth.

Rion reaches into his pocket and pulls out a syringe. "Toradol. To take the edge off the pain."

I shake my head. "No, man. I need a clear head."

"Cutter, you were just shot. Stop trying to be a macho asshole and take help when it's offered."

Even if I wanted to move to stop him, I can't. He picks up the IV line and pushes the needle into the port.

He flashes me a satisfied grin, one that says *I just fucking won.* "Sleep. You need it. I'll come back later to give you another dose of antibiotics and more of the good stuff if you want it."

If I want it...

I don't. And he knows that. He's one of the handful of people in this world who can truly understand what I've been through, how I've suffered, and why I never want to go down that road again. What the drugs do to me.

But he's also probably right...at least for now.

I wave my hand at him. "Don't give me any more of that shit."

His dark eyes meet mine. "I got you, brother."

Within a minute, a familiar fuzziness starts to edge its way into my body, and the pain slowly melts away. "Shit. That *is* good stuff."

He laughs, and his footsteps move toward the door. "Just rest. Leave everything else to us."

What the hell does that mean?

I want to ask, but I can't seem to find any words or move my mouth. The blackness I just managed to drag myself out from under returns, spilling over the edges of my vision. I don't bother fighting it.

What's the point?

The suffocating heat of summer in the Iraqi desert permeates the Humvee. It's like being roasted alive in a fucking tin can.

You never get used to it, but being drenched in constant sweat stops bothering you after a while. Even so, it sure as shit will be nice to get back to HQ and wash off the sand and sweat the last few days have left over every fucking inch of my body.

What I wouldn't give for a cold fucking beer…

I swipe my hand across my forehead to keep the sweat from dripping into my eyes and watch the desert pass as we make our way south. One more brief stop, and then we'll be back to the FOB—the only thing that resembles civilization around here. It can't come soon enough. It's time to get home and get my dick wet. I've spent way too long here this time.

The tiny village appears in the distance, poised at the base of the hills that cut across the middle of the desert. It's always been one of the favorite stops for the guys in the convoys, and it signals how close we really are to being done with this mission.

I glance over at the driver. "In and out. Five minutes. We deliver the boxes, then we go. Got it?"

The young man nods and returns his focus to the road. Even looking away for a second can be deadly out here. Between the IEDs and militia with rocket launchers, convoys like ours are under a constant threat of attack.

All seems quiet, but that's usually when the shit hits the fan.

That strange tingle in my spine has been insistent today. I can't quite put my finger on the cause, but I won't be ready to relax until my feet hit American soil.

The Humvee in front of us pulls to a stop outside the village near the well. Every time we come to one of these places, the locals try to rush the trucks, but I told the guys to keep them back since I haven't been able to shake this feeling the entire mission.

Even though we've been by this village at least a dozen times with nothing happening, it only takes once...

I climb from the Humvee, out onto the hard, cracked earth as the rest of the convoy comes to a stop behind us. The men file out. In the Stryker two vehicles back, the sniper remains on the turret, ever-vigilant even as his Ranger brothers grab the boxes from the trucks and approach some of the villagers waiting on the other side of the low brick wall we use for crowd control.

If we can keep them behind the wall, I'll feel a lot better about this.

Two minutes. In and out.

The guys from the unit manage to keep the villagers back, but three kids slip past. The little boys rush up to me, asking for something in Arabic I could understand if I wanted to listen, but I ignore them and continue to scan the surroundings for anything or anyone out of place.

One of the men comes and ushers the kids away before handing each of them a piece of hard candy from his pocket. Bribery works wonders here—in many forms.

A familiar woman approaches the line of men and points toward one of the guys standing near the Humvee behind me. She's the village chief's daughter if I remember correctly. He's usually with her when we make these stops, but I don't see him today.

Odd.

She always brings us something to drink or eat when we pass by, and I haven't missed the way the men react to her. I'm surprised they don't spontaneously combust or jizz in their pants. She's a beautiful woman with a quick smile and a soft, lyrical voice. No doubt she has suitors lined up outside her family's home already.

One of the men waves her over, and she walks toward the vehicle behind me, holding a box, just like every other time we've stopped here. My hand tightens on my weapon, and I scan the crowd, but nothing seems amiss. Villagers chat with the men; kids run around kicking a soccer ball.

Still, it's time to get out of here.

"Mount up! Let's fucking roll!"

The men hand off the boxes while the Ranger behind me chats with the woman like a smitten dumbass. He doesn't stop grinning for a second, and the rest of the guys pile back into their vehicles.

The Rangers I'm with are great fucking guys and some of the best soldiers. They usually don't do anything stupid, but this guy is completely unaware of his surroundings. A pair of pretty eyes and a smile is all it takes to make him oblivious. He should be watching the villagers, watching the mountains, keeping alert for anything even slightly off.

She glances up and down the convoy and steps forward to offer him the box with a shaky hand.

Why is her hand trembling so badly?

Something isn't right. She shouldn't be nervous.

He reaches for the box.

"No!" My scream carries across the short distance between us, but it's too late. He takes it from her, and her terrified eyes meet mine…

Just before the world explodes.

But it isn't her face this time…it's Valentina.

TEN

Valentina

A throbbing beat pounds relentlessly at the door of my brain. I've donated blood before, but a transfusion is something else completely. It has utterly and totally wiped me out. When Rion was cleaning up the graze on my arm and wrapping it, I was having a hard time staying alert.

The delicious cookies and juice Rion and Grace gave me helped a little bit, but even hours later, I still feel...off. I lean back in the stiff wooden chair next to where they operated on Cutter only hours ago and scan the warehouse for the millionth time since I dropped here.

They offered me somewhere to lie down to sleep, but there's no way I'm closing my eyes and turning my back on these people. I value my life too much. I need to stay alert and on the ball. I need to make sure I pick up any tidbit of information they may offer about what happened with *Il Padrone*.

A door opens somewhere down the hall toward the back of the warehouse, and footsteps echo off the concrete floor as someone approaches. Preacher appears with Milo following close behind him.

The dog bolts straight for the room they took Cutter into and whines outside the door. Preacher reaches down, scoops him up, and mumbles something to him that I can't hear from across the room. Rion looks up from his phone where he sits at the other end of the large table, drinking his third beer, and nods at Preacher.

My hands tighten into fists on my lap.

What are these guys up to?

Any desire to assist them I may have had when Cutter was dying vanishes as soon as the man they call E wanders out from down the same hallway and comes to stand at the side of the table.

I'm vastly outnumbered by men who are two to three times my size, who have nasty reputations and nasty histories, and who undoubtedly don't have my best interests at heart. They accepted my presence last night because they needed me to keep their friend alive. Now that it's over and he's going to make it, any use for me is gone.

That makes them very dangerous.

Rion rises to his massive height and whistles loudly. The shrill sound bounces off the metal rafters, and I wince. He blows me a mocking kiss, and a moment later, Warwick appears at the top of the stairs with Grace.

He stares down at Preacher, Rion, and E and gives them a nod before turning to say something to his girl. Her soft eyes widen slightly, and she shakes her head, but he places his hands on her shoulders and leans in to whisper something. She frowns and narrows her eyes at him before she disappears into their room.

O cazzo.

Warwick doesn't want her to witness whatever is about to happen. That's probably not a good sign for me. It was only a matter of time before they started questioning me. I appreciate the respite they did give me after the transfusion, but they have a job to do as much as I do. And if the roles were reversed, I would start the interrogation while my captive was still weak. It's the easiest chance of breaking them.

But I won't break.

My secrets are my own.

The leader of this band of bad boys trudges down the metal staircase and across the vast expanse of the warehouse floor. Preacher approaches and sets Milo onto the floor in front of me. He trudges right over to Cutter's room, but this time, no one stops him.

That poor dog. Terrified for his owner.

Warwick grabs a chair, spins it around, and straddles it in front of me. "So, Valentina…"

I nod and force a saccharine-sweet smile. "So, Warwick…"

His lips pull back to show off his pearly white teeth. "We need to have a little talk."

Little talk…

I snort-laugh. "What would you like to talk about?" *Murder. Betrayal.* "There are so many options."

Any humor or friendliness he may have been feigning melts away. Something cold, dark, and hard overtakes his stare. "How about we start with who the fuck you are?"

He's direct…straight to the point. I like this guy. It's clear why *Il Padrone* had such a soft spot for him and why what Arturo did to them angered the old man so much.

I sit up straighter in the chair. "I told you who I am. Valentina."

The corner of his mouth turns up slightly. "Do you have a last name?"

"I do, but I'm not giving it to you."

He scowls. "I saw you with *Il Padrone* a few months ago, and I found it very odd that a female would be guarding that man. So, who are you, and why did he trust you? Were you his lover? His girlfriend?"

I snort-laugh and shake my head. "No. Just his bodyguard."

And a pretty shitty one, at that. The man ended up with

more holes blasted through him than Swiss cheese. I could have prevented it if I had just stayed on that damn patio…

Warwick considers me for a moment, steepling his tattooed hands in front of his mouth. "And what about Arturo? Are you fucking him?"

My skin heats and blood rushes in my ears. I would jump out of the chair and deck him if I could. Maybe pistol-whip him if they hadn't taken my gun. "That slimeball could fall off the edge of the Earth for all I care. I wouldn't touch him with a ten-foot pole, let alone let him stick his dick in me."

Rion, Preacher, E, and Warwick all chuckle, and it releases a tiny bit of the tension in the room.

"You fuckers better not be questioning her without me."

The three men in front of me turn, and I shift to the side to look over Warwick's shoulder.

Cutter leans against the doorjamb with his hand pressed over his shoulder and an IV stand next to him. He looks like utter shit, but at least he's alive. That means there's still a chance to get what I want from him. Milo stands at his feet, staring up at his owner, lovingly.

He clearly doesn't know Cutter very well.

Rion glares at Cutter and points toward the room. "Go back to bed. We can handle this."

Cutter's lip curls, and he pushes off the doorjamb. Each step he takes toward us makes me wince. That man is in pain —a lot of it—but he's determined, and he's not going to let it stop him. "I told you fuckers not to question her without me."

Warwick raises his hands. "We're not interrogating her. We're just having a friendly conversation."

The men chuckle again, and Cutter's eyes shift over to meet mine. The storm brewing there sends a chill down my spine—the mix of nothing from the cloudy, dead eye and the ice-blue color of the good one.

He turns to Rion. "Where are my glasses?"

Rion nods to the table behind them. "Grabbed them from

your ride. You're going to need a pretty serious detailing job, or maybe just burn the thing."

Cutter swipes his aviators on his way over to us but ignores Rion's comment about the damage to his SUV. All four guys watch him with concern etched on their faces.

Preacher grabs a chair and places it next to Warwick. "If he doesn't get off his feet, he's not gonna make it long."

Cutter lowers himself into the chair slowly and sits back with a wince. Milo settles at his feet, and his big, brown eyes stare up at me in question. "So, what have you learned since you started without me?"

Warwick smacks him on the thigh. "Just that she apparently isn't fucking either *Il Padrone* or Arturo."

I throw up my hands in frustration. "I tried to tell him in the car, but he wouldn't listen."

I can see why they would make that assumption. A woman in a man's world, a world where women aren't permitted, period. Unless it's as playthings. The mob isn't exactly known for being welcoming and treating females like equals. It's the last place someone like me should end up...under normal circumstances. But the situation with the Marconis is anything but normal.

Cutter presses his lips together. "Why did *Il Padrone* bring you on?"

Lying might be smart in this situation. Yet, I've learned over the years that the truth is usually the easiest answer if you can give it. "Because he said I was the only one he could trust."

Il Padrone suspected Arturo was up to no good; he just didn't know there was already a target on his back. We both believed Arturo was only lining things up to take over when *Il Padrone* died. We never thought Arturo would go rogue and take *Il Padrone* out.

It's hard to read Cutter when I can't see his eyes, but the firm set of his jaw tells me my answer isn't enough to appease him. He expects me to spill. Having five hard and deadly men stare you down might crack most people, but I'm not most people.

Cutter shifts forward in his seat. "And it's just a coincidence that you got up and left right before Arturo did? Right before all the shooting?" He scoffs. "Come on. You can't expect us to believe that."

I shake my head and narrow my eyes at him. "It wasn't a coincidence. I got up because of *you*. I saw *you* and thought you were suspicious and went to check you out. Shit timing as it turns out. If you want to blame anyone for *Il Padrone's* death, blame yourself. You being there is what led me to leave his side in the first place." I don't bother to hide the ire in my voice.

I don't mind telling him that it's his fault. I suck in a deep breath. It's time to lay it all out. There's no point in beating around the bush. "And don't tell me you were there with good intentions. You wanted him gone as much as Arturo did, so let's not play games here."

The tiniest smirk crosses Cutter's lips. "You've got some balls calling us out like that."

He almost looks impressed. He enjoys a challenge. Well, I'm more than ready to give him one.

I shift forward in my chair, straightening my spine and staring directly at him, even though he hides behind those shades. "Don't pretend you weren't there trying to figure out a way to take out *Il Padrone* and more than likely, *Il Padrone* and Arturo."

It wouldn't make sense for them to remove the old man and leave Arturo, especially after their history with the younger Marconi.

Warwick shrugs and rocks back on two legs of the chair. "I certainly wasn't happy about the way *Il Padrone* treated us over the years, or the things he made us do for the sake of some unfair deal I made with him when I was young and dumb. But

I did owe him. My biggest concern was that Arturo was taking over and slowly supplanting *Il Padrone*. Taking Arturo out was the number one priority, but if we had done that..." he pauses long enough to glance at Cutter before returning his attention to me, "we would've had to take out *Il Padrone*, too."

A sardonic laugh slips from me, and I shake my head. "If you only knew."

Cutter grinds his jaw. "Only knew what?"

I flash him a wry smile. They're so clueless about what was really going on. "What *Il Padrone really* wanted. What he was trying to accomplish. Within a few weeks, he would've been in contact with you about it."

Cutter's hand tightens around the IV pole next to him. "About what?"

My smile fades. We were so close, so damn close to accomplishing exactly what needed to happen to make us all safe. I stare at my reflection in Cutter's aviators. I'd give anything to see his eyes when I finally tell him *Il Padrone's* plan. "About taking out Arturo."

Warwick recoils and scrubs his hands over his face. "Shit."

The other guys react the same way—mumbled curses and frustrated hand gestures—except for Cutter.

He sits motionless. Expressionless. A damn statue staring me down from behind the lenses he uses as a shield.

I clear my throat and continue. "He knew he had trouble on his hands. He just couldn't do anything about it. Too many people within our camp side with Arturo and thought it was time for new blood. They thought Arturo could bring us into the future—more money, more power and prestige—and the ones we could trust were too afraid of him to make a move."

Warwick shoves to his feet. "Well, fuck. It seems we may have underestimated Arturo and the old man. You think Arturo is behind this?"

I nod grimly. "I know he is. After I left the hospital and returned to *Il Padrone's* estate, he already had everyone gathered and was barking orders and instituting new rules and policies like he had this planned for months."

Cutter finally moves, pulling his hand off the IV stand and pressing it to his shoulder. "Remind us again why we should trust you?"

"Because *Il Padrone* did."

He sneers and rocks forward in his chair, a move that no doubt causes a lot of pain, but he doesn't flinch, doesn't acknowledge the fact that he was shot less than twelve hours ago and underwent a serious medical procedure. "And just why is that? You show up out of nowhere and are suddenly at his right hand, protecting him."

He's suspicious.

I can't say I blame him. If I were in his place, I wouldn't believe me, either.

All I can do is tell them the truth, or at least, a version of it. "My mother's family were old friends of the Marconis in Italy. I was a police officer there. When *Il Padrone* began suspecting what Arturo was up to, he asked me to come over because he needed someone he could trust. Someone who wouldn't be swayed by Arturo. Someone who could watch his back and conduct an investigation without drawing suspicion."

Cutter barks out a laugh and immediately cringes and presses his shoulder. "You think you didn't draw suspicion? Look at you, *principessa*."

ELEVEN

Cutter

I t's impossible *not* to look at her. She's stunning. Women like her belong on the pages of an Italian fashion magazine, not in a damn police department chasing down criminals.

I can imagine it wouldn't be easy for a woman who looks like her in a profession like that. All the macho guys throwing out sexist comments and jokes, many probably crossing the line on a daily basis. Yet, something tells me, Valentina isn't the kind of person who would have just taken it.

Oh, no, she would stand up to anyone who got in her way or offended her. Like she's doing with us.

Pretty fucking impressive if I'm being honest.

But that dream—drug-induced or not—was a clear warning. Never trust a beautiful woman. Ever. I heard it loud and clear.

Warwick returns to his seat and glances at all the guys before focusing on our female guest. "So, where does that leave us, Valentina?" He rocks his chair back. "*Il Padrone* is dead. Arturo's in control. We all know that's a very bad place for him to be for *all* of us."

She nods her agreement, and her shoulders relax a little.

"I've been looking for evidence that he was behind the shooting, but I have yet to find anything."

Of course.

Her little mouse game, sneaking into the offices in the dead of night, it makes sense now.

I slap my palm against my thigh. "That's why you went back to the offices last night. Pretty fucking stupid if you ask me."

Her perfect rosebud lips press together. "Nobody asked you."

The response almost makes me smile again. Her attitude is equal parts infuriating and captivating. And that's one fucking dangerous combination.

I sit and watch her for a moment. Silence can often elicit more information than questions.

It doesn't take long before she throws up her hands and shakes her head. "I don't have any choice. I can't go back to *Il Padrone*'s house. I barely slipped the tail Arturo had on me. I was at a hotel, but I had to use my real identification to book the room. Arturo has a lot of connections. It's far too easy for him to find me. That's why I need something to nail him. I have nowhere else to go."

"You'll stay here." Grace's voice floats across the warehouse.

I grit my teeth. The woman has been *nothing* but trouble since the moment we set foot on her ship. Now, she's sticking her head where it doesn't belong...*again.*

She stands at the bottom of the staircase, one hand resting on her tiny baby bump, her soft-green eyes focused on our little gathering in front of Valentina.

I scowl at her. "Excuse me?"

She makes her way across the warehouse floor. "I said she'll stay here. It's the only place she can be safe right now."

"And why the fuck is that our problem?" My question comes out harsh, far harsher than I had intended, but I have little to no patience when it comes to Grace and her inserting herself into our affairs.

She doesn't understand our world. This is no place for a woman, especially one like her. Since she's carrying Warwick's child, her presence is something we've all had to accept. But it doesn't mean I have to do it happily.

"We know nothing about her. We don't know if we can trust her."

Grace continues to stare me down. "I didn't know that I could trust any of you, did I? But I didn't have a choice. This may not be where she wants to be, but she needs to be somewhere safe. So, until we figure out a way out of this, it's the best option."

"The best option for whom?" *Certainly not for me.*

The thought of having this woman around day in and day out, every minute and every fucking second while we look for a solution has my blood heating to a dangerous level. A level that only comes right before something blows.

She's beautiful, driven, a total smart ass, and she's apparently fucking deadly.

The perfect woman. If only I believed she wasn't lying through her teeth to us. There may be *some* truth to what she's said, but it definitely isn't the whole story. Not by a long shot.

And the longer I stare at her, the more convinced I am that she's hiding something big.

Our guest looks from Grace to me to Warwick to Rion and Preacher and E, before she shrugs. "So, where do we go from here? I hide out in this shitty warehouse, and what?"

Preacher leans back against the table and crosses his arms over his chest. "You give me the information *I* need, and I may be able to find the information *you* need."

Rion nods at Preacher. "He's pretty good at finding things people don't want found."

Valentina crosses her arms over her ample chest. "You

want to work together?" Her eyes dart around at the entire crew. "That doesn't sound like the best idea."

Warwick stands and tosses his chair to the side. "I think Preacher has the right idea." He approaches her and stops with only inches between them. He squats in front of Valentina and tilts his head to the side. "The enemy of my enemy is my friend, right?"

She scoffs and chuckles to herself, though I have no idea why.

Warwick raises his eyebrows. "What's so funny?"

Her eyes meet mine over Warwick's shoulder. "He probably has no idea where that's from."

I fight against the smug smile that threatens to spread across my face. The guys chuckle behind me, and we all wait for what we know is coming. She's about to eat humble pie.

Warwick lifts one shoulder and lets it fall casually. "Well, the first written record of the phrase comes from the fourth century B.C. in India. Kautilya, who is often referred to as the 'Indian Machiavelli' wrote about the idea in the Sanskrit military book, the *Arthashastra*."

Suck it.

Watching Warwick show off his superior intellect and education to people who only see his tattoos and gruff appearance always brings a kind of joy I rarely experience.

Her eyes widen, and she sucks in a shaky breath. "Wow. I, uh—"

I reach out and slap Warwick on the back. "You thought we were all bunch of idiots thugs, huh?"

Warwick gives her that arrogant grin of his and slowly rises to his feet. I grab the back of my chair and try to stand.

Try being the operative word.

My legs wobble, and I tighten my hold on the back of my chair to steady myself. E reaches out to help me, but I bat his hand away. "It's time to sleep, but later, we start trying to figure this thing out." I wrap my hand around the IV pole and drag it two steps with me before I stop and glance over my shoulder at Valentina. "Someone put her in the storage room."

Grace's mouth drops open, and she looks at me incredulously. "What? You can't make her sleep in there. It's a goddamn storage room."

I growl at her. This is precisely the type of behavior that makes Grace's presence here untenable. "I can make her do whatever the fuck I want."

Warwick glowers at me and holds up a hand. "Watch it, Cutter."

Pussy-whipped asshole.

He's never going to accept that the tension between Grace and me is never going to let up. Not after all the trouble she caused for us and the way she pulls Warwick's strings.

Valentina stiffens her spine and clenches her fists at her sides. "I'm not sleeping in a damn storeroom."

Warwick sighs and glances between Grace and me. I curl my lip at him. It's a warning. One he should recognize means not to fucking push me on this.

He shoves a hand back through his dark hair. The war of being torn between his woman and me batters his resolve, but eventually, he gives Grace an apologetic look and turns back to the subject of my demand. "Sorry, Valentina but our sleeping accommodations are limited."

I give them my back and shuffle toward my room, Milo at my heels.

E sidles up next to me. "The closet? You're really gonna lock her in a closet after she saved your life? Pretty cold, even for you, Cutter."

I pause and turn to face him. "She only had to save my life because I took a bullet saving hers. That bitch can stay locked up in there forever for all I care. We'll deal with the rest after we all get some fucking sleep."

The sound of a chair sliding against the concrete has me looking back again.

Valentina is on her feet now, glaring daggers at me from across the room. "Did he just call me a bitch? That asshole."

A large wall of muscle—better known as Rion—blocks her from advancing. He holds up a hand and presses it to her chest to stop her, and she leans to the side to glower at me.

Rion shakes his head. "Don't even think about it, honey. You will be our guest in the storage closet this evening. Anything else can be hashed out tomorrow."

She huffs and gives me a glare that's probably withered the balls of lesser men. "He called me a bitch."

"He needs his rest."

Hearing Rion tell her that hurts almost as much as this damn gunshot wound, but he's right. If I don't lie down soon, I'm going to drop. I take one final look at her just in time to catch her frown at Rion.

She stares at me but addresses her question to him. "So, he won't be such an asshole tomorrow?"

A deep rumbling laughter from Rion floats across the warehouse. "Oh, no. He'll be worse when he feels better."

I continue the shuffle to my room, ignoring the gibe.

"Lovely."

With that final word from Valentina, I slam my door on that clusterfuck.

I n the harsh light of morning, things don't seem any better. The pain radiating through my arm has me gritting my teeth as I use my left hand to push myself up into a sitting position in bed.

Milo whimpers next to me, raises his head, and cocks it to the side, examining me.

"I probably look like shit, buddy. But I'll be okay."

There's no other choice but to be okay.

The IV line lodged in my arm has helped keep me hydrated after the transfusion, but I'm done with this bullshit. I rip it out and let it dangle from the stand next to the bed.

I'm not some fucking invalid, and I'm not going to stay in bed and take it easy. There's no time for that, not when something this big just happened and not when we have *principessa* locked in the closet.

She better still be there.

"If anyone let her out…" I growl and swing my legs off the side of the bed.

My head swims, and I drop it in my left hand and scrub the stubble on my face. It takes a few seconds for the dizziness to subside, but when it does, I push to my feet. I wobble and grab the IV stand for support.

Fuck.

I actually feel surprisingly good considering what went down, but Rion's also probably right that the smart thing to do would be to stay in bed and take it easy today. But I rarely do the smart thing. At least, that's the way it has seemed since I was discharged.

We need to figure out what the hell is going on with Arturo and that little woman. Her story is too vague; it has too many holes. She's holding something back about *Il Padrone* and protesting her relationship with Arturo far too much.

I stagger over to the dresser and pull down the sweatpants someone dressed me in yesterday. My hand shakes as I snatch a clean pair of gray sweatpants and a T-shirt from the drawer and set them on the top.

The bedroom door flies open, and Rion looms in the jamb. "I thought I heard you staggering around in here." Milo jumps off the low bed and trots over to him. Rion scoops up Milo and eyes me. "How you feeling?"

I grab the sweatpants and slowly step into them and tug them up before I turn to face him. "A little off, but I'll be fine."

Rion nods towards the IV bag and the line loosely dangling from it. "Probably feel a lot better if you were still getting some fluids."

I shrug and immediately regret the decision when red-hot pain stabs my arm. No fucking way that shirt is going on. I swipe my shades from the floor near the bed and step toward him. "Hard to get shit done when you're attached to a pole."

He laughs and steps back so I can leave the room. His eyes drift down to the bandage. "You're not gonna let me take a look at that?"

The right answer would be yes, but there's no time to be fucking around, worrying about something that's probably totally fine.

I shake my head. "Let me get some coffee in me and figure out what the fuck is going on, and then, you can poke and prod at me all you want."

"Ooh, that sounds fun. Careful what you wish for."

Fuck.

Rion has never been known for having the gentlest hands. He's one damn good medic, but being damn good and being gentle are two different things. He saved my life once...now twice, though. So, I guess I need to cut him some slack.

I make my way down the hall toward the kitchen and main warehouse with Rion carrying Milo behind me. "Where is everybody?"

"War and Grace are still asleep. Preacher's in his cave, trying to see if he can locate anything on Valentina with the additional info she gave us last night, and E went for a run."

I nod. I would've gone with him if it weren't for this damn hole in my arm. "And the girl?" I glance over my shoulder.

Rion smirks. "Still locked in the closet. Per your instructions."

"Good. I don't trust her."

He chuckles. "You've made that very clear." He follows me into the kitchen and sets Milo down before he leans back against the counter and crosses his ankles and then his arms over his chest. "I gotta tell you, Cutter, I don't think she's lying to us."

"She may not be lying, but she's not telling us the whole truth." I grab the decanter of coffee with my left hand and pour some into the mug sitting on the counter. I take a sip of the scalding liquid before I settle across from Rion.

"That may be true." He nods. "But don't we all do that? When's the last time you were one-hundred-percent-honest with somebody or volunteered information that wasn't necessary?"

I chuckle at the absurdity of the question and take another sip. "I'm the wrong person to ask."

Rion barks out a laugh and pushes off the counter. "I know. That was my point. Everybody has a reason for doing what they do, saying what they say. You've lived your entire life based on lies. Maybe she's the same." He shrugs. "But she seemed genuinely distressed about *Il Padrone*. I don't think she's involved in his death, at least, not willingly."

Me either.

As much as I hate to admit it, I heard the true despair in her voice when she talked about him and about Arturo's betrayal. She cared for the old man, and I don't think she wished him any harm.

I set down my coffee and watch Rion grab a dog treat from the bowl on the counter and give it to Milo. That chubster grabs it and devours it right there.

Maybe Rion's right. Maybe this girl isn't a spy or some huge threat to us, but there's only one way to find out.

I wait for Rion to rise from scratching Milo. "I'm going to interrogate her."

Rion raises an eyebrow at me. "Isn't that what we did last night?"

I shake my head. "You know that wasn't an interrogation. That was friendly questioning."

His dark eyes narrow on me. "So, you're gonna water-board her?"

A chuckle slips out from between my lips, and I take a sip of my coffee. "Not a bad idea. She'd probably sing in two seconds flat."

He laughs and bends to scratch Milo on the head again. "You're probably right. But do you really want to do that? Is it necessary? Maybe you just need to not treat her like shit, and she might open up to you?"

Christ, he's trying to make it sound like some damn Hallmark movie...

Open up to me?

I slam my mug back down on the counter. "What I need is the goddamn truth about who she is and why she was with the Marconis. Once we have that, we can decide how to approach the raid Arturo is sending us on and where to go from there."

"There's always only ever one way to go, Cutter."

"Oh, yeah, what's that?"

Rion shrugs. "Forward."

TWELVE

Valentina

The door to my cell flies open, and broad shoulders occupy the entire space between the doorjamb. I tug the thin blanket they gave me around my shoulders and shift on the cold, hard concrete floor I slept on last night. Or, at least, *tried* to sleep on. I don't think I closed my eyes for more than twenty minutes at a time.

Cutter stands motionless, blocking the door. Those damn sunglasses cover his eyes, but they're on me, assessing me, measuring me up.

I may have saved the man's life with that damn blood transfusion, yet that doesn't seem to matter to him. I am the enemy. It's the only way he can see me right now. Even after revealing *Il Padrone's* plan, how he wanted *their* help with taking out Arturo, he still can't trust me.

"Get up." His words are cold and harsh like the damn closet I was in all night.

If I didn't know any better, I would swear he put me in here on purpose, knowing how cold and uncomfortable it would be, knowing I wouldn't be able to sleep a wink. Given his training, he must be a master at breaking people. This was a calculated move on his part.

I scowl at him and cross my arms over my chest. "No."

His lips twist into a sneer, and he strides forward and reaches down with his left hand to grab my upper arm. For someone almost dead a little more than a day ago, he's sure moving and acting like nothing happened at all.

The big guy was right, though. He said Cutter would be worse today, and I can already feel the anger and resentment rolling off him in violent waves. He tugs me to my feet, and I jerk against his hold, but his fingers only dig harder into my skin.

"Stop it." He jerks me again. "I wouldn't have to be rough if you weren't fighting."

Coglione! What am I supposed to do? Let them do whatever they want to me? Let them walk all over me? No way.

I'm strong. Resilient. I made it through the police academy and that macho world intact. I'm tougher than I look, and I have a job to finish. That's why I was protecting *Il Padrone* in the first place—I never quit. But I sure failed him.

How could I have been so stupid not to see it coming?

I should have been more forceful. I should have *insisted* we not eat at Moretti's anymore. The man was as stubborn as a mule and pigheaded. It's how he got so powerful, but it's also what brought his downfall.

Even though he knew what Arturo was up to, or at least suspected it, he didn't act. He chose to bide his time and wait for the proof he needed. It ended up giving Arturo an opening. One Arturo took with deadly consequences.

If I give these guys an opening or show any weakness, they'll jump on it. But fighting them won't help me, either. I need them to talk.

I suck up my pride with a gulp of chilly air. "I'll come with you."

His death grip on my arm loosens slightly as he pushes me forward out of the room. We move down the long hallway Rion walked me through last night, past several closed doors that must be bedrooms, and out into the main warehouse.

In the full light of day, I'm finally able to get a good look at the place. It must be an old fish processing warehouse or something. A yacht and some sort of boat sit at slips on the far side of the vast open space, but the main area is sparse except for the big table in the center they used as an operating room.

I glance over at Cutter's arm. Red blood seeps through the bandage there. I shouldn't care, yet the question doesn't go away. It sits on the tip of my tongue as we walk until it finally slips out. "How is your arm?"

He grunts and shoves me forward. The bulldog that was underfoot last night trots toward us from the table. Rion and the quiet blond guy occupy two of the chairs.

Cutter releases my arm, drags out a chair, and points to it. "Sit."

I cross my arms over my chest and stare him down, or I should say, stare at my reflection.

Rion nods at me. "You best do what he says."

He did warn me last night, and he was right.

I huff and sit on the hard, wooden chair.

Cutter scans the warehouse. "Where are War and Grace? Are they *still* sleeping?"

The blond guy points toward the staircase leading up to a room suspended above the warehouse floor. Warwick's room. It's where he and Grace came from yesterday, too.

Something unintelligible but definitely not complimentary slips out of Cutter's lips before he turns to Rion and the other guy. "Keep an eye on her. I'm going to wake them up."

Rion chuckles. "You have some sort of death wish waking up a pregnant woman?"

Cutter snarls at him. "Grace knew what she was getting into. She chose to be here. This is just part of that."

The big guy shrugs. "It's your fucking neck."

My cranky captor storms away and up the staircase,

leaving me with the other two and the bulldog at my feet. He stares up at me with concerned brown eyes, and I reach down to scratch between his ears. A rumble vibrates in his chest against my leg, and he pushes against me harder.

"You're a good boy."

"Milo." The blond guy points to the dog. "His name is Milo."

I look down at the dog. No need to tell them I already knew his name. "What's such a cute, harmless animal like you doing with this bunch of thugs?"

Rion chuckles and shakes his head. "He's Cutter's dog."

I know, and that's even more strange. Cutter doesn't seem like the type to be selfless enough to take care of anything that relies on him for everything.

A door slams and footsteps thunder down the stairs.

Cutter makes his way across the room with his jaw clenched. His focus dips down to where my hand sits on Milo's head, and his lip curls into his trademark sneer. "Milo, come."

Milo trots around the other side of the table and to his owner. The dog is nothing if not loyal. Cutter drops into a chair opposite me and lets out a deep sigh. His face tenses into a wince—one so minor, the other guys may not have even noticed it unless they were watching for it—but I see it.

He's in pain. Being up walking around, dragging me all over the place. It's a lot for him to be doing after what happened. He should be resting and recovering his strength, but he won't let that weakness show. Not in front of me. Not in front of them.

Niall was right—this man is lethal. He's cold, calculating, and a goddamn killing machine. One look into his eyes without the protection of those damn glasses told me that.

There's no reason to get on his bad side any more than I already have. These guys may have wanted *Il Padrone* dead, but I don't think they had anything to do with it. If they had,

Arturo would have gone down with him. A killer could be a good ally.

Steps sound behind me, and Warwick appears, hair ruffled, pulling a T-shirt on. He glares at Cutter. "You and I are gonna have a talk later."

Cutter doesn't respond, just continues to stare at me through those damn glasses. "We don't have time for this bull-shit. We need to figure out what the fuck is going on so we know how to move forward."

Warwick nods and yells. "Preacher. Get the fuck in here."

A door slams from somewhere down the hall, and Preacher makes his way toward us with a slight limp. "All right, all right, I'm here." He takes a seat at the table. "What's going on?"

Cutter leans forward and rests his left elbow on the table while his right rests on his lap. "Arturo wants us to get another shipment for him. Have you been able to find anything, Preacher?"

Preacher shakes his head. "The *Marcella Marie* is out of Rio, and their last three stops were the Suriname, Curacao, and the Dominican Republic. It looks like the particular cargo he's after may have been picked up in the Dominican Republic."

Unease stirs in my stomach. This definitely wasn't a ship-ment of anything *Il Padrone* was aware of. I had a list of what was coming in and when, and none of this rings a bell.

Cutter's mouth tightens into a thin line. "The same port the items from our last raid for Arturo came through, and we know they came from Central or South America before that."

Preacher nods. "Exactly."

Warwick slams his fist against the table. "Fuck. Now that he's in control, he's picking up right where he left off with his plans."

It seems like the guys may know something I don't. I probably shouldn't interject myself into their conversation, but they have me out here for a reason.

"What plans?" I shift forward in my seat. "What is it you think he's doing?"

Warwick's eyes cut over to Cutter, and Cutter gives a curt nod. Warwick clears his throat. "You already know he had us take the shipment of heroin a few months ago. It's why he had Grace and me held at his house when you and *Il Padrone* found us."

I nod. The old man was definitely not happy when he discovered that Warwick and the girl were being held and the reason why. But he was never able to find out what was in the cargo, only that Arturo had ordered it, and was unhappy that some of it hadn't made it to him.

"It was heroin? *Il Padrone* would never touch drugs."

Warwick nods. "You're right. He wouldn't, but Arturo would. He's been making moves to step into the drug market-place for a while."

It fits with what I overheard in the meeting. I just never anticipated he had already started making those moves. "*Il Padrone* knew he was up to something, and that he was making deals behind his back. That's why he brought me on—to be his eyes and ears. To get information and places the other men couldn't."

"Why did he trust you so much?" Cutter's question tightens my chest.

I shrug and try to appear as nonchalant about it as I can. "Like I said last night, our families go way back. He brought me over and figured since I had no real connection to Arturo, I could be trusted. I'm also a cop, or, at least, I was."

"What do you mean *was*?" Warwick steps up beside me.

"Let's just say I pissed off the wrong people, and when I couldn't be bought, I lost my job."

I'm not getting into it with them. The specifics. The fact that my trying to take down *Il Padrone's* competition back home was what got me fired. So much of the force is paid off and under the thumb of the families there. I never knew who was working for us or who I might enrage by getting involved with an investigation. I was just doing my job, shutting down the other families. The fact that it might have ended up benefiting the Marconis was merely an added bonus.

Cutter scowls at me from across the table. "So, you mean to tell me that he inherently trusted you because your families were friends in Italy fifty years ago before you were even born. And he flew you over here to be his bodyguard because of that?"

I nod. "More or less."

There's a lot more in the story, a lot more I can't tell these guys—the ones who would've taken *Il Padrone* out even if Arturo had failed. I can't make the mistake of trusting them when they had a target on his back, too.

Cutter snort-laughs and leans back in his chair. He fights another wince when his shoulder hits the back of the chair, and he uses his left hand to steady his right arm.

Rion glances over at him. "You should really have that immobilized. It would hurt a hell of a lot less."

The only response that gets is a scowl from Cutter and a mumbled, "I'm fine."

The big guy holds up his hands. "Tough-guy asshole." The last word is muttered under his breath but definitely loud enough for everyone to hear, including Cutter.

It doesn't seem to faze him, though.

He continues sitting there with his focus on me. "You're lying. I don't know why. But you are. I have ways to make you talk, though."

Warwick puts his hand on the back of my chair and shakes his head. "You're not doing that to her, Cutter."

"Why the hell not? You were willing to let E and me kill Grace and her crew only a few months ago to secure our safety. This one," he points at me, "is the same threat or even more so than Grace, and you won't even let me perform a little persuasive questioning?"

All eyes are on Warwick now. I glance over my shoulder and up at him. He stares Cutter down across the table. Cutter's implication is clear. He thinks Warwick has gone soft. From what *Il Padrone* told me a few weeks ago, Warwick only got involved in any of this to pay off the family debt. He was rough and maybe a little violent but only had misdemeanors and little shit in his past.

These other guys, though…they seem to be the real deal.

With Cutter's history, or should I say, lack thereof, it means he was top of the top, and if Warwick was really about to let him kill a bunch of innocent people to protect the crew, then what he could do to me during interrogation causes bile to rise in my throat.

I shift forward in my seat. "That's not necessary. I told you the truth."

Cutter's lip curls up. "Maybe a version of it."

"It's the only version I know." I hold the stare I know he's giving me through the glasses. "What else is it you want to know?"

He doesn't hesitate. "If we can trust you to help us take down Arturo."

Therein lies the dilemma. There's no doubt they would have taken out *Il Padrone* eventually, in addition to Arturo, which makes them clear enemies. But after what Arturo has done, they may be the lesser of two evils.

Taking out Arturo myself would be difficult, if not impossible, given the security he has and resources at his fingertips. But with these guys, it might just be possible.

THIRTEEN

Cutter

V alentina considers me for a moment, those too-intense amber eyes boring into mine, even though she can't see them. "We want the same thing, Arturo gone."

Maybe she's finally coming around.

I can understand why she might be leery. We were going to take them both out, and she clearly cared about *Il Padrone*, but things have changed. There's no clear enemy anymore.

We have a common enemy. One *she* can help us take out.

If she opens up.

I shift forward in my chair, trying to find a position that helps alleviate the throbbing in my shoulder. "Any idea who Arturo may have used for the hit?"

She shakes her head. "*Il Padrone* had his suspicions about Arturo, but he never had any proof who he might be working with or what his ultimate plans were."

I snort. "I think his ultimate plan just happened. He wanted *Il Padrone* gone, and he succeeded. He also took out his captains. He wiped the slate clean for all intents and purposes."

"Except for me." Valentina squares her shoulders. "He

didn't know I would leave the patio. I wouldn't have left if it weren't for Cutter."

I flash a taunting grin. "So, I saved your life twice. That means you owe me."

She scowls back at me but doesn't say anything because I'm fucking right.

Warwick slams his hand on the back of her chair. "Will you two stop, already? Christ, you should just fuck and get it over with."

We both recoil, and she turns and glances up at him with an icy glare.

I don't know what the fuck he's talking about. That woman is poison. I sensed it the first time I laid eyes on her at the restaurant. She may be beautiful, but beauty can be deadly. It distracts you from what's really happening, takes you away from the world around you, opens you up to attack.

That mistake can never happen again.

Preacher leans forward and throws his hands up. "So, after Cutter and Valentina fuck, what do we do?"

Warwick glances between Valentina and the guys around the table until his eyes meet mine. "Arturo believes he's in charge. He doesn't know Cutter was there. He doesn't know what we were planning. He also doesn't know we have Valentina. We go get the shipment, and we use the delivery as an opportunity to do what we've always intended."

Take that motherfucker out.

It's all I've thought about since the day War called that meeting to tell us it was time to do something about the Marconis. The fact that Grace's pregnancy was the catalyst to finally get the ball rolling is about the only good thing to come from that clusterfuck with her.

Now, all eyes are on me. Warwick may be the leader of our group, the one who brought us all together and into this life, but I'm the one who does the planning. I'm the one who has the experience and training to get the job done, hopefully, without anyone getting hurt on either side. If blood has to be drawn, I'd rather it be theirs than ours.

I nod to Preacher. "Tell us what else you found?"

He flashes a concerned look at Warwick. "Not a whole lot solid, unfortunately. The *Marcella Marie* has a crew of thirteen, including the captain, and surprise, surprise, it is owned by a holding company that's owned by seven other levels of holding companies. There are so many layers of cover-up here, it's pretty clear a whole lot of shady shit is going down."

I don't like this.

I shake my head. "This is sounding an awful lot like what happened with *Neptune's Daughter.*"

Warwick stiffens at the mention of Grace's ship. He looks between Preacher and me. "You guys don't think this could potentially be related to that heroin shipment, do you?"

Preacher's mouth presses into a hard line. Something bad is coming. "Here's where it gets interesting, or maybe I should say problematic?" He pulls a piece of paper out of his pocket and waves it around. "I tracked that shipment back even further, looking for a connection to any of the holding companies tied to the *Marcella Marie*, and guess what I found?"

I lean forward and rest my palm against the table. "I don't have a fucking clue, but I'm guessing it's not good."

"Well, put it this way. What's been the single biggest fuck up in all the years we've done this?"

I groan. "*Neptune's* fucking *Daughter.*"

He nods. "Exactly. So, imagine my surprise when I discovered a relationship between one of the holding companies that own the *Marcella Marie* and Grace's father's company."

"Fuck." Warwick's hands tighten on the back of the chair Valentina sits in quietly. "Are you serious?"

Preacher nods solemnly. "Some references to one of the holding companies in her father's books. He was carrying a lot of freight for them in the past. Especially in the last six months to a year before he died."

Warwick steps back and rakes a hand through his hair. "Shit." He glances back toward his room where Grace is probably still sleeping. "Did you find out whose shipment of heroin that was?

Preacher shakes his head. "No, and your line of thinking is exactly mine. Whoever these people are, they're powerful and have a lot of money and are working very hard to hide their identities. We stole heroin from them over three months ago, and now Arturo wants us to go after something else onboard one of their ships."

"Jesus." I scrub my hand over my face and glance at Warwick.

He had no clue. I almost feel bad for him. He's going to have to tell Grace. Three months ago, I might have believed she knew, but after spending this time with her, seeing how innocent and somewhat naïve she is, there's no way she was involved or knew how deep her dad was.

If he hadn't died of a heart attack, who knows how long he would've made it playing this game.

I sigh. "And we never found the money. So, what the hell was her old man doing with it?"

Warwick clenches his fists. "We've gone over everything a hundred times. Grace never found anything suspicious or any large sums that shouldn't be there. They were damn near bankrupt when he died, so I have no clue."

It has to be somewhere, but where the money went isn't our biggest concern now. The tie between Grace's father and this holding company only makes the odds of this raid being a set-up even higher. And it's even more likely the cargo he wants is more drugs.

I glance at Preacher. "What is it Arturo needs us to get?"

He looks at the paper. "Three pallets. Arturo's guy sent me the information that said 'arrangements have been made' to ensure it will be accessible."

I bark out a sardonic laugh and shake my head. "So they have somebody on board, or somebody at the dock paid off."

Not really a surprise.

It's so easy to get things into cargo containers. The random checks they do at ports barely catch one percent of the illegal shit brought into this country. It works to our advantage and the advantage of the Marconis.

I snarl and clench my fist. "And we're just gonna believe them when they say it's gonna be a piece of cake?"

Preacher chuckles. "I know. I was thinking the same thing, but if we have to do this job, we don't have much of a choice but to believe that, do we?"

"Of course, we have a choice. We go in with a plan *A*, plan *B*, plan *C*, a plan *D*—"

Warwick waves his hand. "Yeah, yeah, we get the point. How do you suggest we approach this?"

I shove my left hand back through my hair and grimace when I shift, and pain shoots through my right shoulder. "We go in like we always do, on *The Destiny*. We need to be heavily armed on this one with that size of a crew. Plus, if this is in any way related to the shipment from *Neptune's Daughter*, they might be expecting us this time and have somebody ready and waiting on board." I heave out a sigh. "Look what Grace did to fuck up our plans, and that was all random. If they're expecting us, things could go south exceedingly fast."

Warwick raises a dark eyebrow. "Us? You're not going anywhere."

"The fuck I'm not." I shove to my feet, wobble, and have to drop my hand on the table to keep from falling.

He waves a hand at me. "Look at you. You can barely stand."

"I'm fine," I growl low at him. "By the time we leave, I'll be right as rain."

Rion laughs and shakes his head. "Bullshit, brother. You know

I fucking love you to death, and your badassery knows no bounds, but you lost a lot of blood. That transfusion may have you feeling decent right now, but you need time to recover. You can barely move your arm without wincing. There's no way you're climbing onto the ship and shooting a gun. You'll just be a liability."

Preacher gives me a sympathetic look but nods at Rion. "I agree."

I sneer at him and flip him off. "Fuck you, Preacher. You shouldn't talk. You've never even been on one of these. You have no fucking idea what it takes or what I can and can't do."

He holds up his hands. "And you know why I don't go. But it doesn't mean I don't understand what needs to happen."

I slam my palm on the table. "So, you want to go in there with three? Three fucking guys up against the crew of thirteen that might possibly be anticipating us?"

Rion, E, Preacher, and Warwick exchange glances.

We've been doing this for over five years. Always with four and Preacher here monitoring things and controlling our jamming devices. One man down makes a huge difference, especially when that one is *me.*

"You see what the problem is here…" I scan all their faces. "This is a catastrophe waiting to happen."

"We don't have a choice." Warwick's words are final and laced with the same resignation and apprehension I share.

"If Arturo wanted to get rid of us, what would be the easiest way to do it?" I voice the concern that's been niggling in the back of my mind since Arturo called and ordered us to make this raid. "It would be something like this. Send us on another raid. Tell them we're coming. Set a fucking trap."

Warwick curses under his breath. "Is that what you think is going on?"

I shrug and grit my teeth, immediately regretting the action. "I don't fucking know. I just have a feeling."

"Oh, Christ." Rion rolls his eyes. "Another one of these feelings…"

I bend my head toward him. "When has one ever been wrong?"

They haven't. And he knows it.

Before we raided the *Neptune's Daughter*, I had one. Before the attack in Iraq, I had one. I should've listened to my gut, but I didn't, and look where it got me. Half-blind and scarred and working as a fucking pirate for the Marconis.

I look at each and every one of them. "I'm coming with you. You need me."

They exchange looks. They know I'm right. They can't do this with three guys, and we need Preacher monitoring things from home base. Even if he wanted to go, he would be restricted.

No one challenges me this time. I nod. "All right. Then, let's figure out a game plan."

Preacher grabs a roll of paper from in front of him and spreads it out across the table. "Here are the schematics of the boat from the manufacturer."

"Good." I walk around the table, and he moves out of the way so I can examine the ship that could be our demise. The one that could end the amazing five-year ride we've had.

Shit.

None of this would be happening if I'd been able to take out Arturo and *Il Padrone* even a week ago.

Fuck the timing. Fuck the Marconis.

FOURTEEN

Valentina

T he door to my closet cage opens again, and Cutter leans
against the jamb, watching me through his glasses. "You
hungry?"

My stomach growls in response. "Starving."

Other than what they gave me after the transfusion, I
haven't eaten since I've been here. Which by now must be over
two days. Last night was my second in this cold closet prison.
No doubt another one of Cutter's tactics. Maybe the conversation earlier has softened him a little. Though, he did throw
me back in here after it, so I don't plan on getting my hopes
up for that. Not with this man.

He nods, steps in, and the other guy, the one they call E,
enters from behind him. This one has barely said a word the
whole time I've been here. I don't know what his deal is, but
he gives me an awfully sympathetic look before he helps me to
my feet.

Cutter motions with his left hand. "Let's go."

I scowl as I push past him out to the warehouse. He moves
in front of me, and the telltale bloom of red on his shirt
catches my attention. "You're bleeding again."

He glances down at it as he leads me into a kitchen. "I'm fine."

E follows us in and moves over to the stove where a giant pot sits on the burner. He stirs whatever is in it, then grabs a ladle and spoons it out three servings. One large hand removes the lid off a cast-iron pan next to him, and the wonderful aroma of roasting meat makes my mouth water. It gets added to what he already dished out, and E sets silverware on the counter.

Cutter grabs a bowl with his left hand, stalks over, sets it on the large metal counter in front of me, then repeats the process with another. I glance down at the one in front of me.

Wow!

A fork appears in my line of vision, and I glance up at Cutter who is holding it out to me.

I chuckle and shake my head. "Risotto?"

"How the fuck would I know what it is?" He nods toward his buddy, still at the stove. "He's the cook, not me. I just eat the shit."

I dig in with my fork, taking a little bit of what looks like veal shank and some of the creamy, yellow, saffron-infused rice. The second it hits my tongue, I moan around my fork. "Oh, this is good."

Far better than I thought it would be.

E looks over his shoulder at me. He gives me a curt nod but no other response. Cutter doesn't say anything, either, since he's busy shoveling food into his face.

This is better than what I've had at most restaurants here in the States. It almost tastes like being back home—almost.

An ache forms in the center of my chest. I never thought I'd miss Mom this much. When I came here, when *Il Padrone* needed help, I couldn't have imagined I'd end up in this position. This is not what we had planned. The old man was too smart to let Arturo get the upper hand. Yet, he managed to stage a coup. And succeeded.

And Mom has no idea what's happening, what I'm stuck in the middle of. She deserves to know what happened and to hear it from me.

I swallow another bite and steel my nerves to ask for what might be impossible. "Can I make a phone call?"

Cutter looks up at me for a second, chews, and swallows. "No. Until I'm confident of who you are and the real reason you were with the Marconis, I'm keeping you on a tight leash."

"A leash? What am I, a dog?"

He snorts. "They're called bitches for a reason."

I slam my bowl down and push it away from me. Cutter seems unfazed by my anger, continuing to shovel risotto into his mouth and chewing like he didn't just insult me. Losing my cool might not be in my best interest, but I can't keep this in anymore.

I glance over at E, but he's doing a fantastic job of ignoring us. "How long are you gonna keep this up, Cutter?"

He maintains his stoic expression. "Keep what up?" His jaw works as he chews, then he sets his empty dish on the counter.

"This distrust of me. We're on the same side. It would be a lot easier and a lot more comfortable for me if you treated me like an ally instead of an enemy." It's killing me to say this, but he needs to understand. "You were there to kill *Il Padrone* and Arturo, which gives me every reason to hate you, but I'm willing to look past what you guys were going to do in order to achieve our ultimate goal. The one thing we both want. To get rid of that *bastardo*."

His lips twitch, but he fights the smile. He rests his palms against the counter and leans toward me. "You want me to trust you?"

I nod.

"Then you need to tell me what you've been holding back."

Shit.

I try not to react to his demand. "What makes you think I've been holding anything back?"

Maybe the fact I'm a shitty liar...

He chuckles, low and dark. "If you don't already know who and what I am, you at least suspect it. I can smell a liar from a mile away, and *you* are lying. Maybe what you told us is true, but it's not the full truth."

The *full* truth isn't an option.

I grab my dinner and take another bite while I consider my response. "It's all you need to know. My name is Valentina Bianchi, and I came from Italy to protect *Il Padrone*. I failed. Now let me help you make the man who did it pay." I suck in a deep breath and lay it all out on the line. "You need another set of hands, capable hands, *uninjured* hands." I emphasize the word and watch him flinch. "Take me on that boat with you. I can help. I know how to handle a gun. I was one of the best shots in the department. Let me help you. It'll make this goal a lot easier to achieve."

He opens his mouth, no doubt to retort with some snide comment, but I hold up my hand to silence him. If I don't get this all out now, I might never get it out and may end up in the closet again.

"Once we have whatever Arturo wants off that damn boat, I can help you plan a way to take him and his men out when you drop it off. It's going to be our best and maybe only opportunity."

Thunder rumbles and shakes the metal bracing of the building. The sound matches the anger building in my system. I hadn't even realized it was storming, but the sound of rain pounding on the roof confirms it.

A storm like this will probably make my closet even colder. No way. "I'm not spending another night in that cold, dark closet. Your tricks won't work on me."

His signature sneer returns. "Given enough time, everyone breaks, Valentina. And I haven't even started my tricks yet."

It's meant to be a threat and intimidating, and there's no doubt he has the training to inflict all sorts of unspeakable pain if he were so inclined. But I won't play into his ego by showing any fear. I won't flinch.

I mirror his stance, placing my palms flat on the stainless steel and leaning over it. "Let me help you. I know you're a macho asshole who doesn't want to admit weakness or accept help from anyone, but this isn't just about your life. This is about theirs." I point back into the main warehouse where the other men's voices echo as they go over the attack plan again. "Do you really want to risk their lives, make things more dangerous for them just because you're being stubborn?"

"*Sei proprio una puttana.*" He storms around the counter.

The blood blooming on his shirt is getting heavier and heavier.

Even if it's stating the obvious, I need to warn him. "We need to have that looked at."

My words fall on deaf ears. Cutter turns the corner out of the door without a glance back.

E clears his throat.

I turn to face where he still stands at the stove. I'd completely forgotten he was even here. "I'm sorry. I didn't mean—"

He waves me off and offers me a kind smile, the most genuine one I've seen from any of these guys since I got here. "You did mean it. And it's fine. He needed to hear it. It's good for him to have someone stand up to him, once in a while. Keeps his ego in check."

A laugh bubbles from my chest, and I slap my hand over my mouth so Cutter can't hear me if he happens to be lurking around outside the door. I don't need to give him any more reasons to hate me. "I don't think that ego *can* be put in check."

E laughs and nods. "Probably true."

I swipe a stray laughter tear from my eye and grab the empty bowls to bring them to a sink to E's left. "This was very good. Where did you learn to cook like that?"

He shrugs and starts emptying the remaining risotto into a large Tupperware container. "Columbia."

"I'm surprised Colombians know how to cook such excellent *risotto milanese*."

His hand freezes, and he glances over at me with a smirk. "Not *that* Columbia. Columbia Correctional Institution in Portage, Wisconsin. An inmate named Mario Robatelli was the inmate chef. He taught me the basics, though we never had access to saffron for anything like this."

Columbia Correctional Facility...

He was an inmate.

He was...no...*is* a criminal.

They all are.

These men are exactly the kind of people I was trained to catch and remove from the streets. Yet, I ended up protecting one, and I would have killed for him in a heartbeat. And these men, these pirates, for lack of a better word, are going to be the only means to the end I need.

E finishes packaging up the rest of the food and then leans back against the counter opposite me, crossing his arms over his ample chest. The corner of his mouth tips up in a lopsided grin. "You're a cop. Does that mean we're enemies now?"

Is he reading my mind?

I shake my head and chuckle. "I think going to work for the Marconis removes my ability to judge anyone on criminal activities, don't you?"

He chuckles and nods.

"But..." I don't know why I need to ask, but I do.

One of his eyebrows arches as he waits for me to finish my question. He looks so much like a clean-cut, boy next door that it's hard to image him with these guys, let alone behind bars.

"Can I ask what you went to prison for?"

Something dark clouds his blue eyes, and he stares down at his booted feet long enough, I almost try to sneak out. When he finally looks back up, he releases a sigh. "Homicide."

Of course.

He watches me, waiting for my reaction.

I do my best to school my expression. "How long did you spend in?"

"Eight years."

I whistle and shake my head. "That is a long time, though, homicide would carry a much harsher sentence in Italy."

"There were…" he shrugs, "extenuating circumstances."

His muscular arms crossed against his chest tighten, and his jaw tics. The humor in his eyes earlier is absent now. It's pretty clear talking about this makes him uncomfortable. And I can't really blame him. I stand on the opposite side of the line, or at least, I did until very recently.

He points at me. "Why did you leave the force in Italy to come work for a mobster?"

The ultimate question. The one thing I can't answer.

I grin and shrug. "Extenuating circumstances."

He nods with a smirk. "Touché."

Who would have thought pirates would have a sense of humor?

FIFTEEN

Cutter

$\mathbf{M}$orning light still hasn't touched the sky when I force myself into a sitting position on my bed. The pain in my arm alternates between throbbing and stinging.

Lovely.

I scrub my hands over my face, the uneven, scarred skin on the right side, raising echoes of the dream. The same one I have every time I sleep since Valentina's been here.

The same day.

The same road.

The same soldiers.

But a different woman.

I never thought I'd have to keep reliving it. One good thing about getting my brain rocked by the explosion is that my memories of that day are locked away deep in the recesses of my mind. They only resurface sporadically in dreams. During waking hours, I typically have to struggle to raise them, and there's no reason for that.

Milo's deep snoring breaks the silence of the room, and I reach down and scratch his side. His rear leg thumps, and he rolls onto his back completely, giving me full access to his belly.

"I'd love to stay in bed with you all day, buddy, but we have a job to do."

It's going to take hours to get to where we're supposed to intercept the *Marcella Marie*.

That's good and bad.

Good because the chances of there being any water traffic or anyone around to witness or assist is almost nil. Bad because if this is a set-up, it's going to take us a hell of a long time to get back to anything even remotely resembling safety if we need to get the fuck out of there fast.

"What do you think, Milo? Should I bring Valentina along?"

Milo whimpers and lifts his head to look at me with his big brown eyes. His tongue lolls out the side of his mouth, and he rolls onto his stomach and buries his face again to go back to sleep.

"You're no fucking help."

Even though Warwick, Preacher, E, and Rion all think we should bring her, it's ultimately my decision. As it should be.

When Preacher called us into his office to tell us what he found on her last night, I had thought there would be something, anything to justify my distrust. But everything he found matched what she's already told us.

Valentina Bianchi. Born May 23, 1989, Ponza, Italy. Mother: Esmeralda Bianchi. Employed by the municipal police in Ponza before transferring to Naples. And her immigration paperwork shows she entered the country as a Marconi employee of the scrapyard. They obviously weren't going to list bodyguard to a Mafia Don on the application.

There's absolutely nothing suspicious in her background. Nothing that would warrant the unease in my chest and stomach or the chill in my spine. But I know she's holding something back; I just hope it doesn't get us killed.

Because she's right—we need another set of hands. And if she's willing to offer them, we would be fools not to take her up on it. We'd be idiots to overlook the fact that we have a common enemy and could team up to eliminate him. She knows the inner workings of the Marconis better than any of us do.

We need her.

I drag myself out of bed and look down at the wound. Red blood seeps through the bandage Rion placed there yesterday. I told Rion I was fine, but he said I'm going to keep bleeding as long as I refuse to immobilize it and take it easy.

Shit.

Every time I move, it seems to pull the stitches open. I don't have time for this. I walk over to the dresser, tear off the gauze, and examine it. The redness and puffiness weren't there yesterday.

Fuck.

I'll deal with it when we get back. There's no point in worrying Rion. I re-cover it with clean gauze and tape and pull on a T-shirt—black this time, so no one will harass me about it. I shove on my glasses and run a hand through my hair. Milo continues to snore as I make my way to the door and tug it open.

For the first time in ages, Warwick is up before me and walks out of the kitchen with a knowing smirk. "How you feeling, sailor?"

"Fuck off. You know I wasn't Navy."

He chuckles and takes a sip of some truly delicious-smelling coffee from the mug in his hand. "I know. I just like pissing you off."

I scowl and make my way into the kitchen to get my own cup. "Anyone else up?"

He leans against the doorjamb. "Everyone's almost ready. Rion and E are already loading *The Destiny* and *Calista*. Did you make a decision about her?" Warwick nods back toward where I have Valentina stashed in the closet—with an extra blanket. It is pretty fucking cold in there.

It pains me to have to say the words, so instead, I take a sip of my coffee and let it burn down my throat. "She's coming. We need her."

Warwick grins like he knows something I don't. My empty fist clenches with the desire to smash the smugness off his face. Ever since Grace came into his life, he's become an even more volatile mix of "stay the fuck away from me" and "I'm so content it makes everyone else want to puke." He worries about her, and about the baby, about what their lives will be if we can't get away from the Marconis. I've never imagined that kind of life—caring about anyone that much—but it's turned him into one pretty fucking unpredictable motherfucker.

I don't need his attitude directed at me. "What the fuck is that for?"

He shrugs. "It's just nice to see someone else getting pussy-whipped."

My mug almost tumbles from my hand. "Pussy-whipped?" I glare at him. It's too bad he can't see how pissed I am behind these glasses.

Where the hell did that come from?

Warwick's the one wrapped around Grace's little finger. It's heads and tails different from how I feel about Valentina. She's nothing more than a means to an end right now. A way to potentially get more info on Arturo and get our foot in the door to gain access to him to take him out.

The last thing I want is to spend any more time with her than necessary. I shake my head. "Dude, you're insane. I don't even like her."

He raises his mug to me with a smirk. "Sure, you don't."

The lake is angry today, the water churning and swirling the same way my head is trying to wrap it around this situation with Arturo and Valentina. Everything feels off. Like

I'm missing something important. This weather doesn't help my unease. While storms give us a certain amount of cover, they can also cause complications like what happened with the *Neptune's Daughter*.

But summer on the lake is unpredictable. Squall lines, rogue waves, waterspouts…they pop up out of nowhere and can take down even the sturdiest ships and the most experienced sailors.

I keep my eye on the weather as we approach our rendezvous point with the *Marcella Marie* and the rest of the guys. The cargo ship is exactly where Preacher said she'd be. The threatening weather puts her closer to land than we'd originally anticipated and increases the chances of there being witnesses to what we're about to do.

It has that tingle in my spine strengthening minute by minute.

I don't like this—not one fucking bit.

No matter how prepared we are, no matter how many scenarios we've gone over, no matter how many plans we've made, it still feels like walking into something we should be running away from.

I grit my teeth and steer *The Destiny* across the rolling waves toward *The Marcella Marie*. Warwick, E, and Rion are far enough ahead to fake engine trouble and get the ship to stop to assist them.

Valentina's been surprisingly quiet on the trip, but that's mostly because she's been sleeping for almost all of it. Days of sleeping on the cold concrete floor of the storage room have left her exhausted. I can't blame her for crashing when she has the chance. Even the bouncing of the boat across the waves doesn't stir her.

And the respite from her constant attitude and questions gives me a chance collect my thoughts and to watch the woman who has not only thrown a huge wrench into our plans but who may turn out to be a big asset. The contradiction leaves my head spinning, or maybe that's just the lingering effects of the gunshot.

I haven't felt one hundred percent yet, but this morning, my body is revolting. It doesn't seem to want me to be up and functioning. It's a good thing I don't give a fuck about that. What needs to be done is going to get done.

There's no other option.

I glance behind me to where Valentina sleeps on the bench in the wheelhouse. Her perfect lips part slightly with each tiny, rhythmic breath, puffing out from between them.

Giving a shit about anyone else's comfort is foreign for me, but a tiny twinge of guilt about having her locked up in that closet led me to pull out blankets from a storage container and drape one over her and bunch the other under her head earlier. I can no longer see the tattoo that covers her left arm and wraps up across her back. None of us even realized she had it until Grace loaned her the tank top she's wearing today. The realistic animals and vibrant colors seem to oppose so much of what I thought I knew about her. She's a ball of contradictions.

When I dropped that blanket onto her was the only time her eyes even fluttered since she lay down hours ago, but she rolled over and went back to sleep without so much as a thank you. Not that I should expect one, I guess. It's basic human decency to most people. But I'm not most people.

We're getting close now. It's almost time.

I wipe sweat from my forehead and turn back to her. "Valentina."

She flinches at her name, yet her eyes remain closed.

"Valentina, *svegliati!*"

That does it. She jerks and bolts upright, frantically swinging her head from side to side until she gets her bearings. She relaxes slightly. Her small hands brush her dark, disheveled hair back behind her ears.

The boat rolls over a large wave, and I grip the wheel

harder. Fighting the water is never easy, but with my arm jacked up, it's like trying to wrangle a bull with one hand. "We're almost there."

She glances around the wheelhouse. "Where are the weapons?"

The boat was already loaded when she got on. A move that was intentional on my part. I probably won't ever fully trust her, and the thought of being alone on this boat in the middle of Lake Michigan with her armed wasn't one I was comfortable with.

Yet, I only hesitate briefly before I nod to the bench to her left. "In there." She doesn't do much good as an extra set of hands if those hands aren't holding steel. "Do you need me to go over the plan again?"

She shakes her head. "No. I got it. I stay here while you go on and ensure the crew is contained, then you'll come back to help work the crane to get what we need down on board."

"Good."

It's only a minor deviation from our usual course of action. Normally, E would be with me on *The Destiny* because Warwick and Rion are more than capable of handling the crew until we get on board. But with the potential this could be a set-up, we wanted as many people on board immediately as possible.

The satellite phone rings, and Valentina watches me as I answer the call from Preacher. "Yeah."

Fingers clicking on a keyboard sound in the background. "I haven't heard from them since they boarded. Something doesn't feel right."

"Shit. We're going in."

It's too late to turn back now. I gun it, pushing *The Destiny* as hard as the engines will allow. We cruise across the water for a few miles before the *Marcella Marie* and the *Calista* appear on the horizon.

By the time we anchor next to the *Marcella Marie*, the all

too familiar sound of gunfire rings out over the water. Things definitely went to shit before we even got here.

"Motherfucker." I pull the strap of one of the UMP45s over my head. Pain radiates through my arm at the action, but I push it to the back of my mind. There isn't room for distractions of any kind here. I approach the ladder that will take me up the side of the *Marcella Marie*.

Valentina stands behind me with her hands on her hips. "I'm coming with you."

It isn't a question. The damn woman is demanding it. Like she has some right to dictate how this is all going to go down.

I glance down and growl at her. "You fucking stay here. I don't want to have to watch out for you on top of whatever the hell's going on up there. You just be ready to go. We may have to leave without what we came for."

Though I sure as fuck hope not.

If we don't get whatever it is Arturo wants, we won't survive the fallout. Not this time. We only escaped the firing squad by the skin of our teeth during our last job for Arturo because *Il Padrone* stepped in. We don't have that buffer anymore, and Arturo won't be so forgiving this time. That is if this isn't a set-up to take us out in the first place.

Knowing him, he's probably hedging his bets. Either we get killed, or we get what he wants from the cargo—win-win for him. I, for one, would much rather we live and get what we came for so we can use the opportunity to take him out when we deliver the goods.

Anger darkens her eyes, and she looks ready to launch herself up to the ladder to strangle me, but she bites back her words and lets me climb away from her. Pain slices at me with each rung I move higher, but there's no time to stop and be a fucking sissy. Pain is a temporary state of mind.

I slow as I reach the rail and peek over to get the lay of the land. From where I remain concealed by the hull of the ship, I can barely make out a handful of armed men to my right hiding behind a bulkhead under the wheelhouse.

Given where the sound of the gunfire came from when we pulled up, War, E, and Rion must be somewhere to my left, directly across the deck from the crewmen.

I swing my UMP45 into place and rest it on the edge of the rail. I'm only going to have one chance to get off a shot before they return fire. If I'm lucky and they're poorly trained, I may get off a few rounds before they have time to react. But there are at least four of them I can see and maybe more hiding around the side.

The guys better be ready to get their asses out here and fucking back me up. I steady my breathing and bring the scope to my left eye. My vision might not be what it once was, but I can still take out these motherfuckers.

I get one of them in my crosshairs and pull the trigger.

Crack.

The bullet hits my target square in the forehead, and he drops to the deck. The two or three seconds it takes for his *compadres* to realize what happened is enough time for me to fire off two more rounds—*crack, crack*—and take out two more of them. Another one turns his weapon on me and fires.

A barrage of bullets ping into the metal, and I duck back down to the protection of the side of the boat. Gunfire erupts from my left.

About fucking time those assholes gave me some cover.

With the crew members occupied with the guys, I launch myself over the rail. A stream of bullets unleashes at the remaining crewmen, and I fire off a few rounds and duck behind the bulkhead to the left with Rion, Warwick, and E.

I press my back against the metal and grit my teeth, trying to block out the pain radiating through my arm and shoulder.

Rion flashes me a grin. "About time you showed up. You almost missed all the fun."

"Fuck you, Rion. I just took out three of those fuckers. How many did you guys manage?"

Warwick peers around the edge of the bulkhead before turning back to me. "We can rehash all the details later. We took out two, but E caught a bullet in the thigh."

I glance over at where E sits against the bulkhead with a strip of fabric torn from the hem of his shirt wrapped around his leg. What was once grey is now stained red with blood from the wound.

E winces and shakes his head. "I'm fine."

"Can you walk?" Leg wounds usually spell disaster for a successful retreat, but if we can clean out the crew first, it won't be an issue. There are no guarantees, though, which is why I told Valentina to stay ready.

He nods. "If I have to, I can get out of here."

"Good. How many more are left?"

Rion shrugs. "If Preacher's research is accurate, another seven somewhere. Do we abandon at this point?"

Time to state the obvious.

I turn to Warwick. He's the one who will have the hardest time with this. "We can't leave anyone alive."

Warwick sighs and relaxes against the bulkhead. He drops his head back and closes his eyes. "I know."

He doesn't relish taking lives, especially if they're innocent ones. But there's no doubt these men aren't innocent. What Preacher found and how prepared they are for us proves that. These are either cartel men or Arturo's hired guns. Either way, they aren't on the top of St. Peter's list to enter the gates of Heaven when we take them out. I won't feel a twinge of regret when they're gone from this world.

Warwick shouldn't, either, and when he reopens his eyes, his resolve has returned.

I shift to my feet, keeping squatted behind the protection of the bulkhead. "Let's fucking do this."

SIXTEEN

Valentina

I can only stand still on *The Destiny* so long with the sound of gunfire and shouts of pain coming from above me on the other ship. Whatever's going down up there, it isn't good. Cutter fired several times before diving over the rail during a barrage of gunfire.

The guys brought me here to be another set of hands, another person who knows how to handle herself and a weapon, not someone who is useless, waiting down here. Cutter may have told me to stay put, but it's not in my nature to sit around and wait for something to happen.

You have to make things happen for yourself, and friend or foe, these guys sound like they could use some help.

I throw a rifle strap across my chest, shove a .45 in the holster at my side, and climb the ladder. Every rung moves me closer to the top, closer to whatever the hell is going on up there. The gunfire has ceased, leaving only the sound of my heart thundering in my ears and the slosh of the waves below battering the *Marcella Marie* and *The Destiny*.

Was it really only a few days ago I was sitting in Il Padrone's *office, having a cappuccino with him?*

It feels like years with all that's happened.

Dwelling on what was and what might have been won't do any good now, though. My focus needs to be what I am in control of.

I'm a good shot, but I've never used a weapon while on a boat rolling in the middle of a massive lake that might as well be the ocean.

Calmati, Valentina.

Steadying your heartrate and your hand are two of the keys to accurate shooting. It's one of the first things taught at the academy, and it's something I've always tried to remind myself of whenever I have to pull my weapon.

Several deep breaths help center me, and I reach up and grab the rung at the top with a steady hand.

The eerie quiet on the deck continues, and I slowly inch my head up until I can see over the rail. Three bodies lie to the right—the men Cutter took out before he climbed over. Another man is barely visible pressed against the bulkhead they've been using for cover.

Where are Cutter and the guys?

They must be waiting for something. Waiting to draw the man out. And there should be more. Preacher said the crew had thirteen. That means more danger lying in wait somewhere.

Five against potentially nine left are a lot better odds than four against nine. If Warwick, Rion, and E managed to take out anyone before Cutter got up here, our odds are even better.

Movement to my left has my hand tightening around the rifle. A flash of familiar, dark hair and a tattooed hand. That's where the guys are taking cover—behind the opposite bulkhead. They're trapped there until the lone survivor of the crew up here gets taken out.

They needed a diversion, a distraction, something to pull him out from his cover. I've been told I'm great at distracting men. Let's hope it's true.

I give a low whistle, and almost immediately, the man sticks his head out around the bulkhead to look for the source of the sound. It's the only opportunity Cutter needs. A single shot drops the man onto the deck, and those reflective shades turn my way.

A strange mix of chill and heat rolls over my skin. Knowing his eyes are on me gives me a rush, unlike anything I've ever felt before. It's like diving headlong into dark water, not knowing what's down there—exhilarating and terrifying.

This is very dangerous.

He motions for me to join them and indicates he'll cover me. I climb over the rail and dart across to where they hide, my heart racing with every clang of my feet against the worn metal surface.

I dive behind the bulkhead next to Cutter, and all eyes turn on me.

He issues a low growl. "I told you to stay on the fucking boat, *principessa*."

I narrow my eyes on him. The princess jibe when I just made it possible for him to take out the lone crew member still preventing us from moving forward with our plan is going too far. I don't need him to kiss my ass, but a little recognition wouldn't hurt. "You're welcome."

He scoffs. "For what?"

He can't be serious.

I use my rifle to point to the body on the deck. "For that."

He snorts. "You didn't do shit. It was my bullet in his fucking chest that—"

Warwick shoves a hand between us. "Will you two knock it off?"

I bite back the retort sitting on the tip of my tongue and glare at Cutter while Warwick looks between us like we're bickering children.

Maybe we are.

Never having any siblings of my own, I always wondered

it would be like to squabble with someone I was forced to live with in close proximity when they got on my nerves. This might be exactly what it's like for all I know.

Warwick shakes his head in apparent frustration with us. "There are still six crew members on the ship somewhere. We cleared the wheelhouse before these guys on deck showed up. The rest of the crew must be down below. If you two would stop arguing for two fucking seconds, we can get what we need and get the fuck out of here."

Cutter clenches his jaw. He wants to continue, but despite him probably being the most lethal of this bunch, Warwick is their leader. "Let's go take care of business."

I glance over at E and the bloody makeshift bandage he has wrapped around his thigh. "Are you okay?"

E nods and offers what's probably meant to be a reassuring half-smile.

Rion motions toward E's leg. "It didn't hit any arteries or anything. If it had, he'd be dead already."

Cutter wipes the back of his hand over his forehead, swiping at the sweat beading there. It's warm today, but not hot enough to be causing that, and a man like that doesn't get nervous. He turns to E. "You and Warwick stay here in case anyone appears. Valentina, me, and Rion are heading below to take care of the rest of the crew and find what we need. When I give the all-clear, you two head to the boat and get the crane ready."

It's a simple plan. But it's the only one we have right now. Unless they want to abandon the mission completely, but it seems as though they've rejected that idea. Probably for the same reason I won't—getting what we came for will give us a shot at Arturo.

And I'm not stopping until he's paid for what he did.

The man who has caused me nothing but trouble since the moment I saw him across the street in that damn park glances around the bulkhead toward a door that must lead to the lower holds where they store the cargo. He motions for us to follow him and moves out onto the deck.

Quick, sure steps carry us over the open expanse, with Rion covering our rear and Cutter in the lead. He reaches the door and listens for a second before pulling it open and entering.

Cutter moves with such assurance, without an ounce of hesitation. I've seen some pretty incredible cops and soldiers at work, but the stone-cold way he carries himself and his focus are on another level completely. He has that swagger that screams *deadly*.

Thank God he's on my side.

The slightly ajar door is somewhat ominous. Goose bumps pebble across my skin. Cutter looks back at us, motions for us to have eyes on him, and indicates he's entering and we should follow. A dark stairwell leading down to the lower hold greets us immediately inside the door. Cutter doesn't even pause before making his way down into the unknown.

We've got six more people down there somewhere, and any one of them could have a gun trained at the bottom of the staircase, waiting for their chance to take us out.

Every tiny sound—the metal steps creaking beneath our feet, my own blood thundering in my ears, our breathing—all make my hand tighten around my gun. Even with all the raids we did on various organized crime and drug dealers and criminals back home, I don't think I've ever been this nervous about going into the unknown. Although it might simply be my proximity to the man in front of me. He unnerves me in a way I can't even describe. One look from the man who hides his eyes is enough to send my heart skittering in my chest. The combination of attraction and rage mixes into a volatile concoction just waiting to combust.

We reach the base of the stairwell, and Cutter pauses and listens. A faint rustling to the left of the stairs is the only thing I can hear above the sound of my own breathing. Dim light filters from the same direction, enough to make out a few pallets directly in front of us but not much else.

He motions that way to indicate he hears the movement, too, then gestures for Rion to remain at the base of the stairs. Rion nods his understanding, and Cutter indicates for me to follow him.

Cristo. Here we go.

Storming into the unknown. This is probably something he did daily without a second thought, but for me, it's going to take every ounce of training and resolve I have.

Cutter moves around the corner and unleashes a torrent of gunfire in the direction we heard the rustling. I follow as a hail of bullets comes at us, and we both duck behind a pallet of boxes across from the staircase.

Rion remains at the base of the stairs covering our backs. My breath comes out in hot, heavy pants, but Cutter is absolutely still and silent next to me. Heat radiates off his body, and when my shoulder brushes against his, even through two layers of fabric, it practically sears my skin.

He's too hot, but there's no time to consider what that means before he leans into me and motions across the room. He reaches down and grabs a screw lying on the ground and tosses it the opposite direction from the stairwell.

And it works like a charm.

They focus their fire there, and Cutter and I come around the other side of the pallet and unload on them.

It's like watching a master painter at work. Only, instead of sure brushstrokes weaving together to form a beautiful painting that will last generations and elicit a depth of emotion from those who see it, Cutter's art is killing.

I almost feel bad for the people he's unleashing it on.

We duck behind another pallet. Now that our eyes have adjusted to the dim light emitting from a single bulb in the center of the massive storage area, I can make out five bodies on the other side of the room.

There's one more somewhere.

Cutter spots them too and signals for me to get behind him as we advance toward that side of the room while taking cover behind the piles of cargo. We move like a well-oiled machine, like unit members who have worked together for years instead of two people who barely tolerate being in each other's presence. We pause behind a pallet and listen for any sign of the lone crewmember still alive.

The room is silent. Drawing him out is our only option.

It worked up on deck...

I issue a low whistle again, and gunfire slams into the pallet we're behind, this time, from the right. He wasn't with his buddies, but now that he's exposed himself, it's only a matter of a millisecond before Cutter takes him out.

Cutter moves lightning fast around the pallet, and the bullets hit the crewmember in the center of his chest. He drops like a ragdoll against the metal floor.

Jesus. Watching someone kill shouldn't be so fucking sexy.

SEVENTEEN

Cutter

_____

W arwick maneuvers the last of the pallets onto *The Destiny* while I lean against the rail and try not to pass the fuck out.

Fuck.

The longer this day goes on, the worse and worse I feel. The pounding headache started almost as soon as I boarded the *Marcella Marie* and has only worsened as the afternoon has worn on.

A headache I can deal with, but the alternating feeling like my body is on fire and then freezing coupled with the dizziness I've never experienced before has me ready to topple over.

I have a fever. There's no doubt about it. Even with the strong, cool breeze blowing across the water, my body is burning hot, even to my own touch.

Shit. It's been a long fucking time since I felt this bad. I just need to get home.

Once I can lie down, I'll feel better. This will all pass. Rion may need to give me an antibiotic or something, but it's nothing to worry about. It can't be. I turn my face into the wind—anything to help cool down the fire raging in my body.

A loud *thunk* from my left draws my attention. Valentina assists Warwick with securing the last of the cargo, and I stagger over to the winch to pull up the anchor so we can get underway.

At least the water has calmed down a bit since we first arrived. We should make the return trip a little easier than our trip out here. And that's good news because we need to get out of here fast before anyone comes to examine the ghost ship and finds the entire crew decimated.

Thirteen bodies. Thirteen people who died for some stupid war Arturo created. Thirteen people who didn't need to lose their lives but were too dumb to walk away from this life.

Watching my brothers in arms die was always soul-crushing. They were fighting for something. These men…all they were after was money. They made the choices that put them here, risking their lives for the cartel or the mob. Either way, their idiotic decision won't weigh on me.

With Rion already on his way back to the warehouse with E, it's up to us to get the cargo and ourselves back in one piece. That's the only thing keeping me upright at the moment.

As soon as the anchor's up, I turn back to Valentina and Warwick. He moves past me into the wheelhouse, but she just stands on deck, watching me.

Her eyes narrow on me suspiciously. "Are you okay?"

"'Course I am." If okay means barely standing, bleeding from torn stitches, and boiling from the inside out. I might as well be running in full gear out in the desert again with as hot as I feel.

She considers me for a moment, her gaze raking over every inch of my body. "Are you sure because you don't look so good." She leans to the side and stares at my shoulder. "You're bleeding again."

No shit.

I ignore her comment and brush past her on my way to

the wheelhouse. If I stand near her to talk, she'll notice how off I am.

Warwick watches me as I lean against the control panel and move the boat away from the *Marcella Marie.* "She's right, man. You don't look so good. You sure you're okay?"

Not at fucking all.

I glance back at where Valentina remains on the deck, her dark hair whipping around her as she stares out at the water. Warwick should probably take over for me in this condition. I motion toward the controls. "She's all yours, Captain."

"What's going on?" He takes the controls and glances over at me.

I stumble back and drop into one of the captain's chairs behind us. "I'm not feeling very good. Pretty sure I have a raging fever, which means—"

"Which means your wound is probably infected."

More like definitely.

I nod, tug up the arm of my shirt, and pull away the dressing to look at the wound. Blood trickles from the slightly opened skin where the stitches tore, and the puffy, red flesh looks pretty fucking angry. I press my finger to it.

Fuck that's hot and hurts like a motherfucker.

"Yeah, definitely infected."

Warwick grits his teeth. "And you felt fine before we left?"

I shrug and grit my teeth. I have to stop doing that. "Guess that depends on your definition of fine."

He snorts. "You fucking asshole. You never should've been with us if you knew you didn't feel well."

"I was well enough to take out those asshats back there, wasn't I?"

I've never let my partial blindness slow me down. There's no fucking way I'm going to give a little infection that power, either.

He scowls at me and glances back toward the deck at Valentina. "And I'm sure your macho routine has nothing to do with the gorgeous, badass, supermodel cop out there, does it?"

As much as I hate to admit it, her work today was impressive. And with E down, we might not have been able to do it without her. Still, that's not anything I'm willing to confess to Warwick, or anyone else, for that matter. He already has enough fodder for jokes. "No, it had nothing to do with her."

He chuckles and shakes his head. "Whatever you say, brother." His focus returns to the water for a moment before one corner of his mouth quirks up. "Is this what I was like after we took Grace?"

"Like what?"

"Totally and completely oblivious to the fact that I wanted her? Willing to risk my goddamn life just to act like a tough guy in front of her?"

"I'm not doing that."

No fucking way.

His head whips toward me, anger flashing in his almost black eyes. "Oh, you're not? Because it seems to me, we're about eight hours from the warehouse, and you have a raging infection that we're not going to be able to treat until we get there. That's a long time, and knowing you, it's probably been going on since we left, which means it's been destroying your body for at least the last twelve hours. Did you tell Rion before he left with E?"

Fuck. I knew he'd ask, and he won't like my answer.

I shake my head and wave him off. "He's got enough to worry about with E. He doesn't need to worry about me, too. I'll get some antibiotics when I get back."

He scoffs and flashes me a dark look. "When we get back? If you make it that long, you mean…"

He's exaggerating. It's not that bad.

I've had infections and fevers before. None of them have killed me yet. "It's nice to know you care so much about me, but I'm fine."

His hands tighten on the controls, and he stares ahead for a moment before glancing over at me with a tight jaw. "This is really fucking stupid, man. Really stupid. I didn't save your life just so you could throw it away."

I knew this was where it was going, and the fact he feels this way about something I'm doing gives me pause before I respond to him with what was originally going to be a glib remark. I owe him so much more than I can ever repay. I don't want him to think I don't appreciate it.

Not when I owe him everything.

Sucking up my pride is probably the thing I enjoy least in this life, but for Warwick, I'll fucking do it. I reach out and squeeze his shoulder. "You're not getting rid of me that easily."

We aren't the type of guys to hug and get all deep into feelings and shit. This is about as close as we get to sharing anything, but he doesn't need more.

None of us do.

He knows what he did for me. How he dragged me from the hell I had existed in after the attack. Locked away alone under the weight of the dark depression that had become my everyday life and feeling sorry for myself because of the useless monster I'd become.

War didn't need to help me. We weren't all that close growing up. He was just the guy who dated my little sister, who seemed pretty cool. The three years between Nicole and me meant we ran in different crowds, and after War and Nicole split, I barely saw him at all. Yet, he was the one who showed up. He was the one who figured out what I needed and how to reach me. Nicole couldn't handle my anger, the outbursts, the way I pushed her away. But Warwick...he pushed right back, and it was exactly what I needed—a purpose.

I force what I hope comes out like a smile. "I'm not going anywhere."

A wave of dizziness rushes over me, almost as if to say *don't be so sure, asshole.*

Warwick shakes his head. "Better not, you motherfucker."

My hand tightens on his shoulder as the dizziness threatens to topple me.

He motions toward the bench against the wall. "Sit down before you fall."

"Yeah, yeah." I stumble back to the bench where Valentina slept only a short time ago.

Her soft-jasmine scent still lingers on the cushion beneath me. It's been so long since a woman other than Grace has been close enough for me to smell anything so feminine, my cock responds with a twitch.

Knock it off.

I manage to get myself under control and drop my head back against the wall behind the bench. It feels so damn good to sit down; I heave out a deep breath. The door to the wheelhouse opens, and the cool breeze that flows in sends a shiver through me.

Valentina glances at me as she closes the door behind her. Concentration etches little lines around her mouth. "You don't look very good."

"Gee, thanks."

She stands in front of me. "You felt warm earlier when your shoulder brushed against mine. You have a fever?"

Warwick snorts. "Of course, he does. And he more than likely did before we even left to head out here, and he didn't tell Rion or Preacher."

"Of course, he didn't." She glances back at Warwick. "How long until we're back at the warehouse?"

He shrugs. "If we make the best time ever, maybe seven hours. If the weather turns or there's any other sort of issue... longer. And I don't know if he has that much time."

I scoff and raise my left hand. "Oh, Jesus Christ. I'm standing right here."

Warwick glares at me over his shoulder. "No, you're not. You're barely sitting up with a raging infection, destroying your body." He looks to Valentina and motions to the other bench in the wheelhouse. "There should be first-aid stuff in there. See what you can find that might be even remotely helpful right now until we can get him back to Rion."

She nods. I sigh and close my eyes as I drop my head against the wall again.

This is going to be a long fucking ride.

A few old aspirins are all that stand between me and potential death.

S omething cool and damp presses against my forehead, and I release a little moan.

God, that feels good.

I shift on the bed and try to push myself up. A small but firm hand presses me back down.

What the hell?

I open my eyes, but instead of the slightly tinted view of the world that I get from behind my glasses, the stark realization that they aren't on slams into me as I stare up into Valentina's concerned, dark-honey eyes.

She pulls a wet washcloth from my forehead and sets it on the floor next to her. The corner of her mouth quirks up into what almost resembles a smile. "How are you feeling?"

Like fucking hell.

I try to ease myself up again, but she pushes me back down with a force that belies the soft, feminine beauty of the face looking down at me.

She gives my left shoulder another nudge to ensure I'm getting the message. "Stay."

My lips part, an argument on the tip of my tongue. I've never done well with being taken care of. Even in the hospital after the attack, the nurses liked to joke about poking the bear whenever they had to come in to give me any medication or check any vitals. I signed out AMA as soon as I was strong enough to. There was nothing else the doctors could do for the damage to my body, and staying in that environment was making my mental condition a thousand times worse.

Those people were paid to take care of me. Valentina... who knows why the hell she's doing it?

She shakes her head. "Now is not the time to argue with me."

I scowl. She's probably right. I haven't felt this exhausted in a long fucking time. Even worse than when I came in with her. I didn't even know that was possible. "So, I'm alive?"

She raises a playful eyebrow at me. "All your breathing and talking sure suggest that."

"Am I gonna make it?"

It's meant to be a joke, but she sits back and frowns.

She nods to an IV line I hadn't noticed in my arm. "Not because of anything you did, but because of modern medicine and the strongest damn antibiotic you're lucky Rion has here."

Well, shit.

The last thing I remember was the rocking of *The Destiny* out on the lake and Warwick pushing the engines as hard as they would go. I must have passed out sometime during the trip back.

I turn my head toward the window. The lack of light coming in from around the curtains suggests I've been out for a while. When I turn my head back, her gaze focuses on the right side of my face. I almost forgot how exposed I am. Her eyes finally meet mine and pierce into me.

The same ones that stared back at me in my nightmare.

I know it wasn't her in Iraq. I know it was the woman from the village who had been forced to assist with the attack. It wasn't Valentina handing the soldier the box as a signal for them to fire the RPG because all the men were back at the trucks. But even though I logically know it wasn't Valentina, my body still tenses as I hold her stare. "Where are my glasses?"

She glances to the side of the bed. "They're right there."

I reach down and fumble for them.

She catches my hand and holds it in place, stopping me from acquiring the only shield I have against her penetrating gaze. "You don't need them."

"Oh, really?"

Her bottom lip disappears underneath her teeth as she contemplates something. "You can hide behind those damn things all you want, Cutter Jackson, but you can't hide from me. I see you. I see exactly who and what you are."

"Oh, yeah? What's that?"

Many women have tried to unravel me over the years, but not a single one has ever come close. I haven't let anyone get near enough to ever actually know me—for their protection as much as mine.

She leans down, stopping a few inches above me. "You're a man who has fought an impossible war, who has done things that would give normal men nightmares. Things people like me can't possibly comprehend but things that were necessary to protect your people and your country." Her lips are mere inches from mine. Her warm breath fans my face. "You're a man who will do anything for his friends. Even go on a mission when you have a raging infection trying to kill you." She moves even closer, so close, her floral scent completely envelops me, stirring my cock to life. "A man who, despite his best efforts, has somehow managed to convince me he's not a complete and utter asshole."

Well, damn.

I open my mouth to attempt to formulate some form of response—though I have absolutely no fucking clue what it would be—but she presses a finger to my lips. The salty taste of her flesh hardens my cock even more.

"Don't ruin it by opening your damn mouth again." She pulls her finger away and leans in until we're sharing breath. "You, Cutter Jackson, are exactly the type of man I should be running away from. Yet, here I am, taking care of you and praying to God you're going to survive for some unknown reason."

She presses her lips to mine before I can even begin to unpack the words she just said. The way she managed to strip me completely bare when I'm the most vulnerable I've ever been leaves me completely incapable of defending myself against her.

The brush of her lips is soft and tender. Not at all hurried or rushed or demanding like it would be were I the one initiating it. Yet, when she pulls away and stills above me, she takes all my breath with her.

She's managed to do something no other woman has in my thirty-plus years on this planet. She's caught me with my guard down. She's managed to work her way in and under my skin.

And that's a very dangerous place to be.

EIGHTEEN

Valentina

Waking up in a warm, comfortable bed after days of sleeping in the cold, dark closet on the hard, cement floor momentarily disorients me.

Where am...

A hard wall of muscle shifts behind me, and the light scent of crisp water and pine that's all his envelops me.

Cutter.

He drags me back against him, and his hard cock presses against my ass. A low groan rumbles his chest against my spine, and he pushes his erection into me harder.

Merda.

I slept with Cutter Jackson last night. Not *slept with* him slept with him, merely slept in the same bed as him, which isn't much better. He was in far too bad a shape to consider anything more than shuteye. That hadn't stopped me from kissing him, though.

What the hell was I thinking?

This is Cutter Jackson. The man who would've killed *Il Padrone* himself if given the chance. Yet, here I am, lying next to him with his strong arm wrapped around me and his cock pressed deep into the groove of my ass. And my body is primed and ready for him.

I glance up at the IV line dangling beside the bed. He must've pulled it out at some point. Hopefully, not before the dose of antibiotics got into his system.

The warmth of his body cradles me, but it doesn't feel feverish the way he did on *The Destiny* or back here last night. This is the warmth a powerful man radiates when you're lying beside him in bed.

And God, does it feel good.

I can blame my little lapse in judgment last night on the adrenaline still coursing through my veins from the raid and his almost dying, but my very real, very physical reaction to him right now can't be so easily brushed away or explained. What he did on that ship yesterday was absolutely spellbinding and sexy as hell. I'm a sucker for a strong, talented man, and Cutter goes above and beyond that to almost superhuman.

There's no sense fighting it. I want Cutter Jackson as much as I hate him.

I shift my shoulder back so I can turn my head to look at him. The faint morning light streaming in around the curtains falls almost like a spotlight on the web of gnarly red, white, and pink scars crisscrossing the right side of his face and neck.

My hand reaches out almost of its own volition and brushes lightly across the destroyed skin on his cheek above his growing beard. His hand lashes out and grabs my wrist so fast, I didn't even see or feel it move until it was already tightening around my flesh.

He doesn't open his eyes, just tightens his hold around my wrist and uses it to push my shoulder back until I'm facing away from him again. He presses my arm across the front of my body, holding it in place tightly. His warm breath flutters against my neck a second before his lips brush my ear. "You really want to ruin this morning by delving into my demons?"

No. Yes. Cazzo, non lo so.

This man makes it impossible to think.

He releases my wrist and slips his hand down across the expanse of my quivering belly to slide beneath the waist of my yoga pants and the thong below. His fingers find my aching core, and I bite back the moan that threatens to claw its way up my throat.

His tongue snakes out along the rim of my earlobe, and I quiver in his hands, even though he's barely touching me. He pushes his cock against me even harder and slips one finger between my wet folds but holds it still. "Or would you rather have my cock shoved into this hot, wet pussy instead?"

Oh, cazzo.

Cutter is hard. Cutter is brutal. Cutter is unforgiving and relentless. And if I let him have me, there won't be any turning back.

Even with that knowledge at the forefront of my mind, I squeeze my thighs around his hand and shift my hips against the finger poised to offer me something I'm so desperately craving.

"Please, Cutter…" It's nothing more than a whisper. A soft plea because I can't bear to say the words loud enough to admit they came from me.

His lips brush my ear again. "Say it louder for me, *principessa*. Tell me what you want me to do."

Oh, God. Principessa.

It used to draw my ire when he called me that, but hearing that word roll from his tongue with his hard body pressed against mine and his finger poised to plunge inside me is fuel for the burning fire of my lust. He can call me whatever he wants, as long as he touches me.

I grip his arm where it's poised between my legs. "Please, Cutter."

He slips only the tip of his finger inside me, then freezes. "Tell me what you want, *principessa.*"

You.

This.

Everything.

I clench my pussy around him and try to shift my hips to take in more, but his other hand grasps my hip and holds me steady.

This has to be agony for him. There's no way lying on that shoulder feels good, but he doesn't seem to care. He seems to enjoy torturing me even if it hurts him. That shouldn't come as a surprise. The man is clearly a masochist and a sadist. How else could he do what he does?

It doesn't matter to me anymore. What or who he is. I just need *him*. "You. I want you to touch me. I want you to…" The words are right there on the tip of my tongue.

His teeth nip at my ear, and his fingers dig into my hip. "Fuck. Me. Those are the two words you're looking for, *principessa*. You want me to fuck you."

God, yes.

I want that so badly. I didn't think I'd crave anything as much as revenge for what happened to *Il Padrone*, yet, somehow, I do.

So goddamn much.

And it's *this* man. The one who drives me absolutely mad with his callous, demanding attitude and insolence toward me. When he has managed to show me an ounce of respect, it's snatched away rapidly so he doesn't have to show even the faintest hint of humanity.

It's like he's been living in the wild without human contact for so long, he's forgotten how it works. That you're supposed to show humility and gratitude and try to treat people like they aren't just something scraped off the bottom of your shoe.

He's an animal. But right now, that's what I am, too.

This, what's happening between us, is nothing but base need taking control.

I need him to *fuck me*. "Yes, Cutter. Yes."

He slips his finger fully inside me, and I groan and clench around it. The heel of his palm grinds against my clit, and I reach down to clutch at his wrist. My nails dig into the skin there, clawing at him, begging without words.

When the syllables finally form together, they come out on a gasp. *"Di più*...I...need more."

He growls in my ear and sucks the lobe between his lips as he plunges two more fingers inside me, filling me and stretching me while rolling his palm against my sensitive clit. Heat and moisture flood between my legs, and an inferno blazes across my skin. It's suddenly scorching in here. Though it's not from his returned fever. It's the fire of knowing how wrong this is, of understanding how much I shouldn't want it, how much I should say no but knowing deep down, I won't.

I can't.

Not when he plunges his fingers into me and draws them out slowly.

Once.

Twice.

Three times.

I squirm against him, needing more, wanting it all. He shifts the position of his hand, and his thumb finds the apex of my thighs. My clit throbs under the rough pad, desperate like the rest of me. I roll my hips against him, and he expertly circles his thumb around my most sensitive place at a slow, torturous pace that matches what he's doing with his fingers.

It's too much and not enough at the same time.

The men were right—he's an expert at torture, and he's demonstrating that right now on me. He could have brought me to release a dozen times already, but he won't. He can't just give me what I desire most.

A low moan falls from my mouth, and he presses his hot lips against the back of my neck to suck greedily at that spot behind my ear that drives me absolutely insane.

How does he know that?

His pace increases as does the pressure of his cock against my back. He rocks his hips in time with his hand until he's thrusting into me from both sides and expertly rolling his thumb in a rhythm designed to send me crashing over the edge.

My body coils tighter and tighter as he works me higher and higher.

Every limb shakes. My breath catches. I clamp my eyes shut against the intensity of the moment.

I'm right there.

Dangling over the precipice of what is sure to be a mind-blowing and much-needed orgasm.

It's right there.

So close, I can almost taste it on my tongue.

I roll my hips back to meet his pumping hand, chasing my release. My head thrashes from side to side as the low tingle starts in my limbs.

His hand stills, and he squeezes my pussy tightly before a low guttural sound rumbles in my ear. "You can have my cock and an orgasm when you tell me whatever it is you've been keeping from me."

NINETEEN

Cutter

My cock throbs and screams its objections as I pull my hand away from Valentina's warm, wet, welcoming body and shift back on the bed. Six damn years. Over two thousand days since I've been with a woman, kissed a woman, touched a woman, felt her touch…and I'm walking the fuck away.

She lets out a startled cry and rolls over as I climb from the bed. I don't look back over my shoulder. If I do, I might be tempted to give her what she wants instead of getting what I need—the upper hand.

"Are you serious?" Her question comes out as strangled as my balls feel right now.

I don't bother to respond because there's nothing more to say on the matter. She knows what she needs to do to get what she wants. I bend over to grab my glasses from the floor and walk to the door without a glance back. There's no need. I know her honey eyes are darkened with anger and clouded with unresolved lust. It's a look I won't be able to resist.

Shoving on the glasses brings the familiar tint to the world, the one that makes me feel like things are normal, even when they're anything but. I yank open the door and step out into the cool air of the silent warehouse. The smell of cooking bacon floats down the hall. E is up, but everyone else is probably still asleep at this hour.

And me...I could be balls deep in that willing woman right now.

"Fuck." I run my hand over my jaw and glance down at my raging dick, tenting the front of my sweatpants. No fucking way I'm walking around all day pent-up like this. Not if I have to be around her. That was supposed to be torture for her, not for me.

I beeline down the hall toward the bathroom, slam the door shut behind me, and crank the water on as cold as it goes. It's the only thing that will shock me out of this and maybe wake me the fuck up from the nightmare I've created.

Despite the fever having cleared and what I almost did to Valentina back there, I still feel like walking shit. My body's been through enough in the last several days to wear out anybody, and my shoulder aches so badly, I don't even want to move it. Maybe I should reconsider Rion's medication offer.

This shit with the Marconis can't end soon enough.

The glasses feel like a ten-pound weight sitting on my face. What was once so comforting and familiar is now something to question since Valentina called me out last night. I pull them from my face and stare down at them. An innocuous object yet one that has been so integral to my life. I throw them onto the counter and rip off the bandage from my shoulder. The wound looks better today, though I don't really care. I can't right now. I rest my palms flat against the cheap Formica. I drop my head down for a second before forcing myself to look at my reflection in the mirror hanging over the sink.

If there's anything I like less than having someone examine me without the protection of those glasses, it's having to do it myself. The thought of smashing every mirror in this place has crossed my mind more times than I can count over the last five years, and it no doubt will continue to for as long as there's still breath in my lungs. I'll never get used to seeing the monster I've become. All the useless, forced therapy and condescending platitudes in the world won't change what happened or how I feel about it. The only thing that broke me from the endless stream of feeling sorry for myself was Warwick giving me something meaningful to do with my life again. And once this is over, once we end things with the Marconis and free him and all of us from the debt…

Then what?

I turn from the mirror and step under the spray. The icy water caresses my skin the way Valentina's hands could be right now. My dick twitches, reminding me of my purpose in coming back here in the first place.

Get it out of your system. Get her out of your system now, and don't repeat it.

There are bigger things to worry about than sexual tension between that woman and me like the fact we took out a crew of thirteen men on that ship yesterday. If no one has discovered them yet, they will soon, and that puts us in a grim position.

We're smart enough to make sure we policed our brass and didn't leave prints anywhere, so the chances of anyone finding anything to connect any of us with what happened on the *Marcella Marie* are slim to none, but that still leaves the problem with Arturo.

They were expecting us. Warwick said the crew was acting cagey and pulled weapons on them almost right away. It was a set-up. Had to be. Which means Arturo never expected us to succeed. He was willing to warn them and sacrifice the drug shipment to take us out. Any façade of a pleasant, working relationship we may have had has shattered. So, getting in and getting rid of him is the only thing that matters.

But that problem can wait for the next five minutes. The more pressing one is squeezed firmly in the palm of my hand.

I give my cock one hard, long stroke and groan under the

fall of cool water. Those little mewls that came from Valentina's lips when I touched her ring in my ears.

The way she said my name...

The way she begged for it...

Her hips rolling against my hand...

All of it. All of her.

It's like fucking crack to me.

I stroke myself again...harder, faster, remembering the feel of her greedy cunt clutching at my fingers. It isn't long before the tingle starts at the base of my spine. I grit my teeth and increase my pace, rotating my wrist and pinching when I reach the head of my cock until it almost hurts.

The orgasm slams into me almost as hard as the damn RPG that almost killed me.

"Fuck!" I gasp as jets of my cum shoot across the tile of the shower and disappear down the drain. God willing, along with any attraction Valentina had for me and I for her. It will only lead to more anger and hurt for her and more frustration for me.

It's bad for both of us, and we're both smart enough to know it. Hopefully, what just happened taught her a lesson. One she won't so easily forget. Tangling with me is tantamount to welcoming a killer into your heart. I'll eat her up, spit her out, and break her down until she's no longer capable of breathing.

And I won't even feel bad about it.

I soap off and wash my hair. Getting the scent of Valentina off my skin can't happen soon enough. The bubbles swirling down the drain give me hope I might have ended whatever the hell this was with my actions back there. If not, I'm well and truly fucked.

The chilly air in the bathroom makes me shiver when I step out of the shower. It's an appreciated shock to the system. The more I can do to snap myself out of what happened, the better.

For everyone.

I grab a towel and run it over my face, hair, and chest and wrap it around my waist as I scan the bathroom.

"Shit."

In my haste to get away from that infuriating woman, I forgot to grab a change of clothes. The too-small towel will have to do until I can get something to wear from my room. I return the glasses to my face where they belong without looking in the mirror again. That's hard enough while clothed, let alone practically naked.

Maybe one of the guys would be willing to go into my room to grab some clothes so I don't have to see her again.

E is up, so there's at least one option. I tug open the door and listen for sounds of life in the hallway. The familiar patter of paws on the concrete floors heads my way, and Milo nudges open the door to get to me. I drop into a crouch and take his face in my hands, scratching behind his ears.

"Hey, buddy."

He snorts in my face, and his tongue lolls out to the side.

"Yeah, I missed you, too. You're a much better sleeping companion than the one I had last night."

It's a lie. He snores and kicks and hogs the bed like he's a mastiff instead of a bulldog, but I won't hurt his fragile ego. He rubs his head against my hands.

"You think she's still in there?"

He looks up at me and tilts his head. He has no fucking clue what I'm talking about.

I stick my head out into the hall and scan both ways. The doors to Rion's and Preacher's rooms are now open. Looks like pretty much everyone's up. Though Warwick is probably still hunkered down with Grace. I roll my eyes and rise to my feet.

If Grace were up, at least I'd have a chance of someone running interference with Valentina without giving me too much shit about it. Grace knows not to push me too far. The guys, on the other hand, enjoy doing just that.

I step out in the hall and move toward the door to my room. It's closed, which means there's a pretty fucking good chance that woman is still in my bed. I suck in a deep breath and glance down at Milo.

"Here's the deal, buddy. I need you to be a distraction in there while I grab some clothes. You know what to do."

His brown eyes search mine, and he gives a little whimper, almost like he understands what I'm asking. And maybe he does this time. There are times where he inherently seems to know what people need. He's been a lifeline for me more times than I can count. Taking care of him and having to get out of bed every day to walk him was what helped keep me alive when Warwick showed up to drag me back to life.

I wince at the creaking of the door as I push it open. The bed is empty, and I release a deep sigh of relief and shove my hand through my damp hair.

Thank God.

One less drama to have to deal with this morning. She won't cause a scene in front of everyone else, not about what happened. And it wouldn't have had to go down that way in the first place if she would have come clean with us from the first minute she got here. Even though she helped us immensely yesterday, I can't shake that niggling feeling she's holding something important back. If she's not going to be honest, I have no plans to help her…with anything.

I tug on a pair of jeans and a T-shirt while I try not to inhale her lingering, sweet-jasmine scent that still permeates the room.

Fuck.

I'm going to have to wash the sheets to get rid of that damn smell. If I try to sleep with that invading my senses, I might never stop jerking off. But first, food. My stomach rumbles almost in time with my thought. "Let's go get some grub, buddy."

Milo dashes off in front of me. That kitchen is his favorite place in the whole fucking warehouse. If anyone is more of a sucker for that damn dog than I am, it's E. The dog eats better than most humans for fuck's sake.

That delicious bacon smell calls to me from down the hallway, and the guys' voices float out the kitchen door. I find them leaning against various counters, deep in conversation. All of them look up at me at once. They stare at me intently, but no one says a fucking word.

I look from Rion to E to Warwick to Preacher. "What? What's the fucking look for?"

Warwick smirks and shakes his head. "What did you do, man?"

That's a pretty broad question. I've done a lot of things in my life, most of which I can never discuss. "What do you mean?"

Rion snorts, takes a sip of his coffee that's likely flavored with whiskey, and offers me a grin. "What did you do to Valentina?"

I scowl and walk between them over to the stove where E stands, holding a plate piled high with bacon, eggs, and toast. I glance down at his leg, but I can't see anything through the sweatpants he wears. A pair of crutches rests against the counter next to the stove. "How are you doing? Should you really be up and around?"

He shrugs. "I'll live."

Warwick chuckles. "Mostly because he listens to Rion."

I snarl at him and dig into my bacon. The second half of the piece goes to Milo. When I stand back up, the guys are staring at me again.

Preacher tilts his head. "But really, man, what did you do to Valentina?"

"Why does everybody keep asking that? Where is she, anyway?"

They all chuckle and drink from their mugs of coffee without answering me. I shovel a forkful of eggs into my mouth and chew, returning their stares.

Assholes.

Preacher finally cuts me some slack as amusement turns up his lips, and he shakes his head. "We keep asking you because we just dealt with one very pissed off woman."

I swallow a bite of eggs. "Isn't that just her usual state?"

He sighs and raises his hands. "Only around you, buddy."

"Where is she?" I'm not sure why I care at this point.

She has nowhere to go and no one to turn to. She's not leaving here. She needs us definitely more than we need her.

He nods upward toward Warwick's room. "With Grace. Using their bathroom."

And no doubt cursing me with every bad word in the Italian language.

"I didn't do anything to her..." They all give me disbelieving looks, and I take a bite of toast and chew it slowly before I swallow. "That she didn't want..."

Rion smacks his palm against the counter. "There we go. *That she didn't want.* When are you gonna learn you can't toy with women like that, Cutter? Has it been that long for you that you don't know better?"

I chew and make him wait for my answer. "Why does it matter? She's gonna be gone as soon as we get the shit with Arturo sorted out. Speaking of which, what's the plan?"

Warwick takes a sip from the mug in his hand. "That's what we were just discussing when you walked in. I think it's safe to say our raid was expected yesterday."

"Gee, you think?" My words are mumbled around a mouthful of toast but still understandable. Which means he glares my direction with great displeasure.

Warwick pushes off the counter and refills his coffee mug.

"Either Arturo told them we were coming, or they anticipated it on their own. We still don't know which, but my money is on him somehow getting them a warning."

Me too.

He moves back to his place against the counter and leans back. "That leaves two different ways to tackle the situation." He holds up a finger. "One, we call him and tell him we got the stuff."

"Is it more heroin?" The question comes from the still fuming Italian beauty standing in the doorway with Grace.

My bite of eggs lodges in my throat. I manage to choke it down. I'm about to say it's none of her fucking business, but after what she did yesterday, I guess it kind of is. She's an accessory to murder now…and smuggling and piracy and whatever else the prosecutor could come up with for what we do. And she's invested in the Arturo situation.

Warwick glances at me before focusing his gaze her direction. "It was more heroin."

They must have opened the pallets last night while I was still out cold with the fever. Heroin isn't exactly a surprise, but the fact that it was actually drugs means the men were likely cartel and received a warning. If they were Arturo's men, there wouldn't have been any reason to use real drugs.

Grace frowns, and Warwick opens his arms for her. She walks into his embrace and rests her head on his chest. Valentina remains, leaning against the doorjamb. Her shimmering eyes bore into mine from across the room and practically melt me on the spot with the strength of the anger in them.

I force myself to eat another bite of bacon and give the rest of the piece to Milo. He takes it and trots over to her and sits at her feet, wagging his tail and staring up at her.

Fucking traitor.

She looks away from me and to Warwick. "And what's option number two."

"Well, option number two only applies if it wasn't a set-up from Arturo. If it was just whoever the drugs belong to protecting what's theirs, then Arturo's probably anticipating us calling and arranging delivery. But if it were a set-up with his men, he would have heard by now from the crew. The fact that he hasn't will probably tell him we survived and got the cargo."

I set down my plates and lean against the counter. "It wasn't his men. They wouldn't have used real drugs."

Warwick frowns. "Good point. So, Arturo sent them a warning somehow, but the crew belongs to the cartel."

"Bingo."

Valentina chews on her bottom lip. "So, what are you suggesting, Warwick?"

He thinks for a minute, running his hand up and down Grace's back slowly. "I think our best course of action is to tell him we got the heroin and use it as a way inside and to him."

Warwick's right. Getting in past Arturo's security won't be easy. Especially after the break-in at his offices the other night. They know something's up, and they'll be on guard. They may try to take us out as soon as we arrive before we even have a chance to get in the same room with him. Even if they didn't get a good look at me, they had to have recognized Valentina, even from a distance. That ass is unmistakable, especially retreating.

And if what she says is true, Arturo wants her gone. He wants us gone. He wants her gone. This could definitely work to our advantage.

I focus my gaze on the woman who is the key to every-thing; I just don't know why yet. "I say we offer him the drugs and something else even more enticing, something that might prevent him from trying to take us out."

Rion scratches at his stubbled chin. "Yeah? What's that?"

I hold Valentina's stare. "Valentina."

TWENTY

Valentina

The fucking *stronzo* wants to use me as bait. As a way to ensure Arturo is going to let us into the compound and close to him.

What a dick!

"Don't let him get to you." Grace's words finally break through the cloud of anger that's been surrounding me since the moment Cutter made the suggestion.

I suck in a deep breath of crisp, water-scented air and stare out at the dark green of Lake Michigan rolling in toward the beach under our feet. I couldn't stay in there without wanting to lunge across the counter and strangle a certain man with aviators.

It's a good thing Grace dragged me out before I did just that. But the fresh air outside and the beauty of the lake are doing little to calm my rage. And it's not merely because of what he did this morning or that he wants to dangle me in front of Arturo like a carrot. It's because he doesn't see anything wrong with either. Not an ounce of regret or concern.

The bastard.

We make our way across a rocky beach toward a lighthouse in the distance. Grace's words rattle around in my head. *Don't let him get to you.*

I stop and bend down to pick up a smooth, flat rock. I glide my thumb across the perfect surface and flip it over in my hand. The other side is pock-marked and jagged like it was slammed against another larger rock and broken by the impact prior to landing on the beach to have the other side smoothed by the tide rolling over it every day. "That's easy for you to say."

She raises a pale eyebrow at me. "Why do you say that?"

Isn't it obvious?

The past few days haven't given me much of an opportunity to get to know Grace, mostly because I spent them locked in that damn closet. But she seems genuinely concerned for me, something I can't say about any of the guys. And she clearly doesn't understand what I'm dealing with when it comes to Cutter. "Because you're Warwick's girlfriend. You're one of them."

She barks a laugh that rings out in the still morning air and shakes her head. "You have no idea."

"No idea about what?"

Her small hand falls to her slightly swollen belly, and a light breeze comes in off the lake, swirling her red hair around her face. "None of these guys are easy, but you're dealing with Cutter who is, by far, the hardest of them. He wasn't exactly welcoming to me, either. In fact, he threatened outright to kill me on more than one occasion."

"What?" Cutter threatening to kill an innocent woman might be the most shocking thing I've heard since being here. "That seems a little bit extreme, even for Cutter."

She chuckles softly and stares off into the water. "Let's just say, my start with the guys wasn't the best. And there's a reason I call that man The Kraken."

"The Kraken?"

The only Kraken I know of is the mythological octopus-

168

type creature that used to terrorize sailors. I'm not sure what the hell that has to do with Cutter.

She winks and chuckles at what must be my confused expression. "You know, the monster from ancient mythology? The unstoppable beast? The killing machine…"

I snort-laugh and shake my head, and we continue to make our way down the beach. "It is a very fitting nickname."

Especially after I saw what he could do yesterday on that ship. He really is a machine. I'm not sure what, if anything, could stop him once he's started down a path with determination.

Grace nods, and a smile tugs at her lips. "Yeah. I would never call him that to his face, of course. I don't have a death wish, but I have nicknames for all the guys."

"Oh, really?"

"Uh huh. I call Rion 'the Hulk.'"

Visions of the green monster flit through my head, and I chuckle as I picture the massive man in the warehouse who seems to flip from hard to soft. "Also, very fitting."

She shrugs. "I think so. He can be fucking mean and use all that brute force in really bad ways when he wants to, but he also has a softer side. The alcohol seems to help even him out, though I would never admit that because it may make him think the way he drinks is normal."

Rion seems to care so much about these guys and does his best to take care of them even when they don't want to let him. Even when they flat-out fight him on it like Cutter has been doing. He's determined and loyal, even if he does apparently drink more than he should.

We pause our walk again and watch a seagull dive into the water, probably looking for its breakfast.

Now that Grace has mentioned it, I can't help but ask about the other guys. "What about Preacher? What's your nickname for him?"

The corner of her mouth tips up, and her eyes soften with

genuine affection. "Priest. Because I've never seen that man touch a woman."

In the few days I've been here, I've barely seen him even leave his room except to eat and meet with the guys to plan something. Walking past his "cave," as the guys call it, I've caught a glimpse of the massive and complicated computer set up. I can only assume he's some sort of tech genius. "Is he gay or celibate?"

She shakes her head and kicks a rock in front of her down the beach. "No, I think he's just a little reluctant to dive into the dating pool; plus, he never really gives himself a chance. He's attached to those computers so much, the only times I see him leave the warehouse at all are to go get some new ink or to grab a drink at one of the local bars with Rion."

There's more to that story, but my curiosity about the final member of the crew beats out my need to ask more about Preacher. "And what about E?"

Her mouth twists, and something dark crosses her eyes. "Elijah is a tough case. I just call him Einstein."

"Because of the *E* name?"

She laughs again, but it doesn't reach her eyes. "I wish it were that simple. E is brilliant. He was a chess champion as a child, and he has one of those minds that could be used for so much good."

Why did a guy like that go to prison for murder?

"What's he doing with these guys, then?"

We approach the lighthouse, and I stare up and watch the giant bulb spin round and round, throwing its beam out across the water every second. I glance over at Grace, who stares up at it with equal amazement even though she must have been out here a hundred times.

She finally glances over at me. "Warwick once told me, the stories are the guys' to tell. If they don't want you to know, you won't. I'm not the one to give you that information, Valentina."

As much as I want to know the background of this ragtag group of men, I can understand their wanting to keep their life stories and secrets to themselves. I haven't exactly been completely forthcoming with them about my life, either. But there's so much I don't understand about Cutter, things that might explain the complicated man.

We continue to walk along the beach, leaving the lighthouse behind us, and I pause to grab another rock from the sand. "It really is beautiful here, isn't it?"

She nods. "It is. I can't imagine ever living anywhere away from the water. I grew up in Michigan and was on the lakes with my dad a lot. Settling this close to it helps me feel like I'm not too far away from him."

Il Padrone told me about her father's death and how she had stepped up to captain his ship, the very one Arturo sent the guys to raid to steal a shipment of heroin, but we never had time to delve into any more details. We were too busy trying to sort out Arturo's dealings and prevent a coup.

I glance at Grace, and the sadness brought on by talking about her father is written all over her pale, freckled face. "What about the rest of your family?"

"Well, my brother is military and has been deployed off and on for the last couple of years. And my mom is basically a homemaker with no one left to take care of. She still lives back in Traverse City."

"What about the family business? If I remember correctly, *Il Padrone* told me that your father had somehow been pulled into transporting something for Arturo."

She nods and wrings her hands in front of her. "After I found out I was pregnant and came back here with Warwick, the guys hired somebody to run the company from Traverse City so that I wouldn't have to have my hands in it anymore, just in case any investigations ever happened. I also think Warwick wanted me to come here without anything holding me back."

Nothing holding her back.

When I left Italy to come here, everything was so rushed, so uncertain. All I knew was *Il Padrone* needed me and had a plan. I never imagined what that plan would be. Now, thinking about returning home brings complicated feelings I'm unsure how to unravel. What's happening here is so important. If I'm truly able to accomplish it, it may be a long time before I set foot in Italy again.

That thought tightens my chest and makes my eyes burn with unshed tears. "Do you miss it?"

"I do, but..." she rests her hand on her stomach again, "my future is here with Warwick."

"Even though he does what he does?"

She presses her lips together in a hard line and is silent for a few minutes as we continue to walk farther and farther from the warehouse. "It was an issue for a while, and I would never say it to his face, but he knows it still bothers me now. The thing is, though, these aren't bad guys. Not really. They do bad things, criminal things for a living, but in their own way, each and every one of them has shown me something good."

"Even Cutter?"

I have a hard time believing that after what he did to me this morning. The lingering effects of his torture still have my body aching and craving him despite how he treated me.

"Yes, even Cutter. He's the one who fought it the hardest and still continues to fight against my being here and my place in Warwick's life, but every once in a while, there's a glimmer of humanity there."

I guess I've seen it, too, if I am really being objective about it. In those brief moments he lets down that wall he's built around himself, it's there. The way he cares about the other guys and is willing to risk himself to keep them safe. It's just so damn hard when he fights it so much.

G race shoves open the door to the warehouse, and I follow her from the bright morning sunlight outside into the vast space. Even walking along the water for almost an hour hasn't done much to cool my temper when it comes to Cutter.

While Grace may be right, there is something good in him, something I, myself saw, the way he played me this morning to get me to tell him what he wanted to know isn't something I can simply forget and pretend didn't happen.

Somebody needs to call him on his shit.

Maybe I'm not the right person to do that, but what does it matter? I'll be gone as soon as the Arturo situation is dealt with and will never have to see any of these guys, especially Cutter, again.

A strange ache forms in the center of my chest with that thought.

What the hell?

I reach up and rub at it as we make our way across the warehouse toward where the guys—minus Cutter—sit around the table. I scan the warehouse for him, and movement on my right stops me in my tracks.

Cutter.

He climbs up the ladder of *The Destiny* and swings his leg over the rail onto the deck. He must be going to check out the cargo. The guys opened it last night after we got back and Rion and Preacher started antibiotic treatment for Cutter. Even though they told us it was heroin, knowing him, he'll want to see it for himself.

Grace stops a few feet in front of me. "Valentina? Are you coming?"

I turned back to find all eyes at the table on me. I should go over there. Find out what the plan is for Arturo—if there is one yet—and stay far, far away from the man who manages to stir up so many emotions in me.

But I don't.

"I'll be there in a minute." I turn and walk over toward the boat slip where *The Destiny* rolls gently in the water.

This warehouse is so immense that both she and the yacht they own fit inside the interior and can be completely unobserved from anyone outside. It's actually a pretty perfect hideaway. They can disappear after a job and make any changes to the appearance of the boats away from prying eyes in case authorities are looking for them.

I stare up at the ladder to the deck. From down here, I can't see Cutter. He's no doubt up there, trying to figure out a way to commit murder. That should give me pause. It should give me another reason to turn and walk away. It should turn my stomach and disgust me. I've spent my life protecting other people from criminals, enforcing the law, and ensuring innocents don't get harmed. Well, most of my life.

How did I end up here? How did I go from a well-respected cop to a mob bodyguard?

I know the answer, but it's one I still have trouble wrapping my head around sometimes. And right now, it doesn't matter why I'm here, just that I am. These are the people I need to help me take out Arturo.

The last time I climbed a ladder like this, it was to commit murder...

And considering how angry I am right now, I may do it again.

Hand over hand, rung after rung, I make my way up and swing my legs over the rail. Cutter stands with his back to me, examining the crates and pallets sitting on the deck.

The lids from the boxes lie strewn around, and as I slowly approach, the packages of heroin come into view.

Jesus, that's a lot of drugs.

It's the one thing *Il Padrone* never wanted to be involved with. He knew he could make a lot of money, but he didn't want his hands dirty in that way. Gambling, no problem. Prostitution, no problem. Murder, no problem. Drugs, no way. He had to draw the line somewhere, and that was it.

Arturo taking that route and going behind his back was the ultimate betrayal. Until he killed him.

"What are you doing up here?" Cutter's deep voice cuts through the silence.

Slow steps bring me forward next to him, and we both stare down at the drugs. "I came to talk to you."

He doesn't turn, doesn't glance my way, but I turn to face him. The gnarled, scarred, right side of his face stands directly in my line of vision. It must have been incredibly painful, whatever caused that. A thousand different scenarios flit through my head, each worse than the last, yet likely none are as bad as what actually happened.

His fists clench at his sides. "We don't have anything to talk about unless you came up here to come clean with me."

Come clean with him. If only it were that easy.

I need their help, which means he can't know everything. None of them can. But maybe there's a way to gain his trust without exposing the truth.

"What you did this morning was a pretty asshole move. When a man touches a woman like that, he better follow through."

He finally turns his head to look at me. A muscle in his jaw tics, and anger colors his cheeks. "What were you expecting, *principessa*? Hearts and fucking roses and declarations of undying love? Trust me, if I ever follow through with you, everyone in a ten-mile radius will be aware."

Oh, mio Dio!

My clit throbs, and the memory of his fingers brushing against it and moving inside me has me clenching my thighs together. His arrogance should be a huge turnoff, but everything about Cutter seems to be a contradiction.

It has a mix of attraction and rage heating my blood. "You really want to know what I've been holding back?"

GWYN MCNAMEE

He sneers. "Of course, I fucking do. We can't go into this without knowing everything. That's how people get hurt or worse."

Here goes nothing...

"Fine. The reason *Il Padrone* trusted that I would come and help him and would never betray him is that I've been doing work for the family in Italy for years."

Cutter doesn't flinch, doesn't react at all. "What kind of work?"

The kind a cop should never be doing. The kind that has weighed heavily on me for a long time...until I learned the truth.

"Before I tell you, I need to explain something."

He snorts. "I bet you do."

"I was a good cop. I worked hard. I took out a lot of bad guys. I made sure innocent people didn't get hurt."

"But you also helped the mafia. Sounds an awful lot like you're making excuses to make yourself feel better."

My lips part to argue with him, but I bite it back because he's right. I am making excuses to justify what I was doing... am doing.

I nod slowly rather than admit it out loud and swallow through the lump in my throat. "Like I said, the Bianchis and the Marconis were old friends. When *Il Padrone* learned I had joined the force in Napoli, he began asking me to take care of things for him here and there."

Cutter raises an eyebrow that just peeks out over the top frame of his glasses. "Things like?"

"Things like letting his people back home know when the police were getting close to busting them or when a raid was going to happen. Like entering false leads from informants to shut down competitors' operations."

"So, he was using the police force to do his dirty work? Using you?"

I shrug, trying my best to appear nonchalant when the

words sting. I hadn't thought about it like that. "Basically, yeah, and as much as I hate to say it, I did it."

He laughs a dark, deep sound that sends a chill through me. "And where were those high and mighty laurels you were resting on? A friend asked for a favor and they just...poof... disappear, huh?"

His words shouldn't hurt me. I've had to live with what I've done for a long time now. Yet, hearing someone with no conscience say it and judge me for it hits me far harder than I could have ever anticipated.

I squeeze my eyes shut against the burn of impending tears. I will *not* cry in front of this man. "It's just not as simple as that." But it's all he's going to get out of me right now. "You asked for the truth, and I gave it to you."

"And why didn't you want to tell us earlier?"

Is he really this dense?

I open my eyes and lock gazes with him as I prepare to admit my biggest shame. "I'm not exactly proud of what I did, Cutter. I swore to serve and protect, and I helped out a criminal enterprise. But I justified it to myself because I was taking out people who were even worse."

He barks out a laugh and shakes his head. "Wow, *principessa*, you sure have a jaded view of ethics."

"Who the hell are you to talk about ethics? Your government trained you to be an assassin. To take out people they no longer had use for, or who they claimed posed a threat, without it being traced back to the US. Now you're basically a gun for hire. What does that make you?"

So much for not being the one to call him on his shit.

He turns to face me fully and steps up into my personal space, his chest almost bumping mine. Heat and anger roll off him in waves as big as the ones we saw out on the water. "It makes me someone you should stop fucking with."

"Me? Fucking with you?" I roll my eyes, drop my head back, and laugh. "You sure have that fucking twisted around. I wasn't the one trying to use sex as an interrogation technique this morning. That was you."

And my body still remembers every damn second of his touch. Every brush of his lips against my heated skin...

He shifts even closer, until our chests touch and I can feel the steady beating of his heart against mine. "Oh no? Then what the hell was that kiss? You did the same thing to me, and you did it first."

"Wow. That's what you really think? That I kissed you because I was trying to get something from you? What could I possibly need from you that you haven't already willingly and freely offered me?" Fury loosens my tongue, and I clench my fists at my sides to keep from using them. "I kissed you because I wanted to. Not as some sort of fucking game." I stare up at my own angry face reflected back at me. I shouldn't say it, I should keep the rest of my tirade to myself, but the words bubble up, and there's no way to push them back down. "And if you would stop hiding behind those damn glasses and viewing the world through their filter for two seconds, maybe you would've seen that. But you're too fucking jaded to even know what's real anymore. Or maybe you never did."

TWENTY-ONE

Cutter

_____

S he doesn't have a fucking clue what she's talking about.
Not. A. Fucking. Clue.

The fact she said that to me should be the final nail in the coffin of anything ever happening between us, but her tenacity and courage are absolutely sexy as hell.

No one stands up to me.

No one.

Yet this woman isn't intimidated. She doesn't shrink away or cower. She has bigger balls than most men I know.

Anger and something even more dangerous boil and rage inside me as I stare down into the blazing eyes of quite possibly the most infuriating woman in the world. She might as well be throwing kerosene on the fire burning inside me.

Despite my best efforts over the last few hours, I haven't been able to get the feel of her body pressed against mine out of my head, or the taste of her skin from my mouth.

Even knowing what we're facing in the next few days and that she'll be gone from my life when we take care of Arturo, I still want her. At least once. Just the thought of her channeling all that passion and anger into sex has had me walking around with an almost constant hard-on even after my solo-session in the shower.

Her fiery reaction to my suggestion that we use her as bait only intensified my need to fuck her into submission.

And I *did* promise her my dick and an orgasm when she came clean.

It probably took a lot for her to reveal all that. To admit she'd been working both sides for years had to have been hard. For someone who pretends to be so idealistic, it turns out, she's as bad as us, if not more so. We don't pretend to be anything we're not. Even though Warwick's fishing company acts as a front for our activities, we are still pretty open about who we are and what we do. At least, we have been with her. And she proved what she was willing to do and how far she would go on that ship just to get Arturo.

She's proving it now coming up here. Staring me down and calling me out. She'll do anything.

She has no idea what she's unleashing.

Her chest heaves, pressing her ample breasts against my thundering heart. I reach out and wrap my palm around her chin, tilting her head up and back. The challenge in her eyes doesn't waver, but her body quivers slightly.

It's not in her nature to submit or give in, but she still wants it as much as she did this morning, even after what I said and did. She has no right to say those words, and even less to expect me to follow through on what we started this morning after those words left her lips. But even my anger can't keep me from taking what I want.

Not when the future is so unknown. Not when she'll be gone so soon.

She squirms in my hold and pulls her bottom lip under her teeth, waiting for me to do or say something.

I won't make her wait.

"One word is all it'll take, *principessa*." I lean down until my lips are a mere hair's breadth away from hers. "One word, and I'll give you what I promised."

Her body vibrates against mine, and those hands she's had clenched at her side for so long reach up and curl around my waist, dragging me even closer and crushing my hard cock between us.

"Cutter."

My name.

One word.

Not the one I was expecting, nevertheless, it's an invitation to take what I want and how I want it.

Right.

Fucking.

Now.

I force her backward until her shoulders and ass hit the wheelhouse, and I press her into it, lowering my hand to wrap around her neck while the other cages her in.

Her amber eyes ripple with desire, but there's a lingering darkness behind them. Maybe because of what I did earlier today. Maybe because of what happened on the ship yesterday. Maybe because of what happened to *Il Padrone* or what I would have done to him had Arturo not taken care of things. Whatever the reason, it disappears in a flash, and it doesn't stop her tongue from snaking out to wet her lips.

Fuck yes, principessa.

I brush my thumb over her throbbing pulse, and her lips part, a tiny gasp slipping between them and unraveling any reservation I have. She's unleashed the beast. There's no turning back now.

My lips find hers—hard, hot, and heavy. She groans into my mouth and tightens her hold on my waist.

This isn't the kiss from last night.

That was a possibility.

This, this is a given.

This is now.

This is *it doesn't fucking matter what comes tomorrow.*

This is pure animal need.

This is all the pent-up aggression and frustration we've felt since her eyes met mine from across that damn street in front of the restaurant.

Her nails dig into my sides as my tongue slips between her lips. The more I taste of her, the more I crave. Sweet, spicy, and flaming hot all at the same time. A lethal combination. One I'm willing to risk my sanity for.

I tear my mouth away from hers and tighten my grip on her neck. "Turn around."

She whimpers slightly but doesn't hesitate. I reach down, unbutton my jeans, and unzip my fly. I shove them down to let my raging cock spring free. From over her shoulder, her shimmering gaze meets mine, and her eyes drop to my left hand wrapped around the base of my shaft.

I reach up and secure my hand around her neck, dragging her back against me and tilting her head to my shoulder. "This is what you want, isn't it?"

She nods and rolls her hips back into mine. I nip at her ear, and she shoves down the skin-tight yoga pants encasing her glorious ass.

My cock hits the hot skin there, pressing between the cheeks, and I grit my teeth against the very real desire to shove it somewhere she's probably not expecting.

God, yes.

I slip my hand between her legs from behind and find her pussy wet and ready for me just like she was this morning.

Fuck!

The scent of her arousal surrounds me, and my mouth waters to taste her fully, but not now. My cock inside her is the only thing on the menu at this moment.

I slowly drag a finger through her wet folds and flick it across her clit. As much as I want to be inside her, playing with her, torturing her is so much damn fun.

The wars inside me rage hard.

Between love and hate.

Anger and lust.

Fear and desire.

She jerks back against me, her body practically liquid in my hands. "*Per favore*, Cutter. Please."

My cock twitches, and I squeeze my hand around her throat. "Please what, *principessa*?"

The words. I need to hear them in that sexy accent of hers.

"Please…" She quivers.

I drag my cock between her legs, coating it in the evidence of how much she really wants me.

She moans and swallows, her throat contracting under my palm. "Fuck me. *Ti voglio dentro di me.*"

Those words vibrating against my hand are exactly what I needed. "You got it, *principessa*." I align the head of my cock with her cunt and shove up inside her in one strong thrust.

"Oh!" She rocks forward. Her fingers curl against the wood of wheelhouse, and she drops her forehead against the wall and turns it slightly to the side, her bottom lip crushed between her teeth.

Her pussy contracts around my cock. Scalding, tight, and wet, just like I knew she'd be.

It's been so fucking long. And this feels so fucking right.

I lean forward and brush my lips against her ear. "Remember where we are, *principessa*. Everyone is thirty yards away, and this warehouse echoes. Remember what I told you? That everyone would know I was making you come?"

She nods slightly and whimpers as I push the tiniest bit further, all the way to the hilt.

"Well, I'm going to prove that." I drag my hips back until only the head of my dick sits inside her pussy. She clenches down around it again, and I grit my teeth.

I've always had unbreakable restraint. In everything. It's

what made me the best at my job. But this woman is so fucking close to cracking me wide open.

So. Damn. Close.

I drive into her again and press my hands over hers on the wall to hold her in place. Her legs shake, and with every thrust, my balls tighten, and a little bit of my anger at her slips away.

Her hips roll back to meet mine. The aggressive pace I've set apparently isn't too much for her. She's eating it up, devouring every inch of me and everything I have to give.

She's so fucking incredible. Everything I thought didn't exist wrapped up in one strong, sexy package. But...she'll be gone soon. Which means I need to make the most of this opportunity while I have it. I may never get the chance again.

I slide one hand down between us and slip a finger into her ass. She jerks and squeezes around me in both places. I brush her thick, dark hair to the side and kiss my way up the back of her neck. "Have you ever had someone touch you here, *principessa?*"

This lush ass was built for it.

Built for me.

I drag my finger in and out in time with my cock, and she bites her lip even harder and shakes her head in a confusing combination of back and forth and up and down. Whether or not she's let someone fuck her in the ass before is irrelevant. Even if she has, I'll be the one she remembers for it.

"I'll get you ready, *principessa.* I want you to feel me here," I twist my hips and shove my cock even deeper in her pussy, "and here," I shift my finger, "for the next fucking week."

Even longer, if she's lucky.

The pace I've set doesn't seem quick enough. I roll my hips faster and harder with each retreat as I maneuver my finger inside her to create friction against the head of my cock on her G spot.

"Oh, God, oh, God..." Her legs shake as her orgasm

builds. Her hands claw at the side of the wheelhouse, leaving tiny scratch marks in the wood. She's about to blow.

I tug her ear between my teeth and bite down, and she detonates harder than that RPG that hit us. Her cry echoes through the high, empty rafters of the warehouse, but she doesn't seem to care that everyone can hear us, and I sure as fuck don't.

Her pussy clenches and ripples around my dick, sending pleasure straight through my entire body.

Sweet fuck.

After everything I've been through, everything I've done in my life, I never thought I would know what Heaven felt like. But it's this. Being buried inside this woman while she gives herself over to me completely.

I release her ear and lick along the lobe as aftershocks from her orgasm wrack her body. She sags, and I use my free arm to wrap around her and hold her steady. I still with my hard cock inside her and give her a second to regain her composure. But only a second. "I want to fuck you in the ass now, *principessa*, and you're gonna come again harder than you ever thought possible."

She whimpers and tightens around me again. Involuntary response or not, it's an invitation I'm not going to decline. We need this. To get rid of this tension between us, this strange mix of emotions. She needs it. I need it. And I'm gonna give it to her.

I pull my cock from her still quivering body and drag the wet head back between her cheeks and over the place I'm absolutely dying to be. She's so fucking wet, I could enter her like this, but I don't want to hurt her. I spit on my dick before rubbing it across the opening again. She clenches, and I lean forward and kiss behind her ear. "Relax, *principessa*. I won't hurt you."

She nods and mewls a little before spreading her legs wider, angling herself up, and offering herself to me.

Sweet fucking Christ.

I push in slowly, gritting my teeth against the tight heat and resistance from her body. She freezes, and I reach around to her clit and roll my fingers against the wetness there to help her loosen up. She relaxes slightly, and my cock slips in even farther.

Inch by inch, she takes me inside her welcoming body.

If I thought she was tight before, this gives the word a whole new meaning. I finally seat myself all the way inside her, suck in a deep breath, and lean forward to rest my hands on hers. With my chest pressed against her back, I kiss across her collarbone to her shoulder. "Turn your head."

She does as she's told and turns toward me.

I kiss her. Harsh, hard, and needy. She squeezes my cock like a fucking vise.

I groan. "You do that again and I'm going to come. I'm not ready for that yet."

She whimpers, and I drag my hips back slowly and push into her in the long, slow slide. Her body shakes, and I reach down and rub her clit again as I start a slow rhythm.

It doesn't take long before my orgasm builds again, a dark, roiling heat in my spine, tightening my balls as I drive into her. I pick up the pace. Faster and harder but not enough to hurt her, even though that might be what I wanted deep down.

My roar as I empty myself inside her echoes through the warehouse, and I pump two more times before I still against her. I press her into the wall, using it to hold up both of our quivering and sagging bodies and brush my lips up her neck to her ear.

"See what good things will come when you're honest with me, *principessa?*"

TWENTY-TWO

Valentina

T he door to Cutter's room creaks open, and light from the warehouse streams in and lands on me where I lie on the bed. Milo trots in, climbs up, and settles near my feet.

Cutter's broad shoulders momentarily block out the light as he enters, then he shuts the door, thrusting the room into darkness except for the streams of moonlight coming in through the open drapes.

It seems like ages ago we were on that boat and he was fucking me—hell, breaking me—but it's only been hours. Hours I've been replaying every word we said and every brush of lips, every damn touch. My body still quivers with the after-shocks and aches in the best possible way from what he did to me...what he took from me.

Cristo.

It was...ethereal. Like being taken to another plane. Another type of reality where all that exists is a strange mix of pleasure and pain that comes together to form something greater than I've ever experienced in my entire life.

The fact that it was a man like Cutter Jackson who brought me there shouldn't be surprising, though.

He, himself, is a strange, complicated mix. Arrogant and

yet deferential to Warwick. Passionate yet possessing an eerie calm even in the worst of circumstances. Strong yet suffering and flawed...

He slammed into me like a rogue wave—suddenly, without warning, and with a force so tremendous, it knocked me from my axis and pulled me under, practically drowning me.

And now, staring at Cutter in the moonlight streaming in, my body stirs along with something far more important and terrifying...my heart.

He watches me silently, his hands clenching into fists then opening again. There's a constant storm raging inside him, one I had hoped might be quelled by what happened earlier today. But the tension is still there, in him, between us, filling the room and the air.

With my back to the windows, he probably can't tell if I'm awake or not, and something about watching him watch me now feels like a betrayal. Like I'm lying to him...again.

I shift up on my elbow and examine him, waiting for him to make a move or say anything in the aftermath of what happened.

When he left with the guys to go pick up some supplies for our attack on Arturo, it felt like he couldn't run away from me far or fast enough. After walking away from the boat without a word, it only cemented my belief that there were so many things left unsaid.

We haven't discussed what happens after...*after* we take out Arturo. The plan is simple enough. They called and advised him they have the heroin and me—two things we know he wants. They offered him a deal, both in exchange for releasing them from their debt. We all know his agreement to consider and discuss the offer was bullshit, but it gets us in the door. Once there, we take action. But even the simplest of plans can go wrong, and the hours they were gone left me with Milo, Grace, and my own thoughts, which can be a very dangerous thing.

Because right now, they're telling me I need to know more about this enigmatic man, who despite everything pointing to him being absolutely wrong for me, feels so fucking right.

He tugs off his T-shirt, his muscles bunching and flexing in the moonlight and highlighting the scarred skin along his right side. My breath catches in my chest. He kicks off his jeans, exposing his muscular thighs and an intricate, colorful phoenix tattooed on the top of the left one.

Rising from the ashes.

Given his scars, it seems appropriate. His cock hangs between his legs. The heat of his stare warms my skin. It stirs to life before my eyes. He pulls back the covers and slips into bed beside me.

We're less than a foot apart, but it somehow feels like miles between us. Too many unspoken words. Too many unacknowledged feelings.

And I'm too chicken to delve into them right now. "Did you get everything we need?"

He nods, and the moonlight reflects off his glasses. My fingers itch to take them off. To throw away the stupid thing that prevents him from letting anyone see or know the real him.

I want him to understand that he doesn't need to hide his injury for me. That it's just part of what makes him who he is and shows his strength, his bravery, his ability to survive anything. While others might be scared or turned off by the sight of the ugly scars, they're what draws me to him.

But if I do it now, reach up and pull off those damn things, after calling him out earlier, after connecting with him the way I did, it might be pushing him too far, too fast.

So instead, I wait and watch.

He can't possibly sleep with those on, can he?

Would he? Just to spite me and make a point?

I lie back onto my pillow while he stays poised up on his elbow, looking down at me. His arm raises, and he pulls them off his face. His hand tremors slightly as he sets them on the floor beside the bed, but whether it's pain from the healing gunshot, nerves, or some other unspoken cause, I don't know.

I never know anything for sure with Cutter.

And that's precisely why I can't turn away.

He's a mystery to unravel. A case to solve. The cop in me can't walk away without understanding what makes him tick, what makes him so angry, what makes him...*him*. And maybe figure out why I'm so damn attracted to such a hard and difficult man.

The simple fact that he's exhibited zero pain or limitation since the raid only adds another mark in the incredible column.

Incredibly brave.

Incredibly strong.

Incredibly tenacious.

And an incredible asshole.

Yet here I am...

Moonlight strikes the left side of his face now, and the damage he tries so hard to conceal from the world remains hidden in the shadows. He must've been a real fucking heartbreaker before the accident. Before he shut out the world and everyone in it except the guys in this warehouse and a dog.

It's stupid, and I shouldn't do it, but I reach up and cup the unmarred skin. I pause for a second, then turn his face so the faint light illuminates his scars. I brush my thumb across his cheek near his dead right eye. For a split-second, he closes his eyes and leans into my touch before his hand snaps out, grasps my wrist, and yanks my hand away.

That minuscule gesture. That single moment in time where he leaned into my touch. It tells me more than any words could.

No matter how much Cutter pushes me, pushes everyone away, no matter how bad his attitude is or how much he reiterates his desire to be left alone, he craves affection. He craves comfort and passion and connection, just like every other person on this planet.

He stares at me for a moment, his jaw hard and lips twisted in a sneer, challenging me to object to his rebuke. Then he releases my wrist and drops his head down onto his pillow.

The question sits on the tip of my tongue, begging to fly out into the silent room. Voicing it may send me back into the damn closet. Even knowing that, I can't stop myself from asking it. "How did it happen?"

It's not my business, and we both know it. Yet, maybe it is after what happened today. I don't know. How can I? How can I know *anything* when it comes to this man except that I can't seem to stay away from him despite all the reasons to?

Despite the biggest reason that he doesn't even know…

He rolls onto his back so he's staring up at the ceiling and the damage to his body is on full display in the moonlight. "Are we really gonna do this?"

"Please, Cutter, I want to know."

He sighs and swallows thickly, his Adam's apple bobbing in his throat. "Iraq. Six years ago…"

I freeze, and goose bumps spread across my skin. His voice is strong and unwavering, but the emotion is so thick, my chest tightens.

He clenches his fist where it lies on his chest. "Joint mission with the Rangers. A village we had been to a dozen times with no problems. The men felt safe. They let down their guard. It was an ambush. Enemy combatants with RPGs were waiting on the mountainside above the village for a signal to shoot when everyone was back at the convoy. It happened because someone didn't listen to me when I warned him. That's why I never hesitate. Because I know these can be the results."

My heart breaks for what he must've gone through. What

his men must've gone through. I blink away the tears forming and swallow through my dry throat. "How many men died?"

"Twenty-seven."

Cristo.

So many men, gone in an instant. It's unfathomable. Yet, Cutter is still here. He made it. "How many survived?"

His eyes drift closed for a second. I reach out and lay my hand across the scarred right side of his chest.

He flinches, then takes a deep breath and relaxes. "Five. Me, Rion, who was a Ranger medic, Preacher, who was working in CIA intelligence at the time, a Ranger sniper named Gabe, and another Ranger named Max."

"Were they injured, too?"

He turns his head toward me and opens his eyes. The light of the moon electrifies the blue of the left eye and glints off the icy pale white one. "Everyone gets injured in some way over there. Some wounds just aren't as visible as mine."

A single tear trickles from my left eye onto the pillow.

Please don't let him see it.

If Cutter sees me crying for him, he will take it as pity and effectively shut any door that may be cracked open right now. He turns his head away from me and effectively ends the conversation. Pressing him any further risks him shutting down completely. But I need him to know I understand, if only in a tiny way.

I brush away another tear. "One of my partners was killed."

Cutter stills and angles his head slightly toward me.

It's an invitation to continue. "I know it's not the same thing as losing that many men, as being in a war zone, as being injured but..." I suck in a deep breath as the memory of that day blasts its way to the forefront again. "It was just a stupid street thug who didn't want to spend the night in jail. Three gunshots to the chest. Mario bled out before help could arrive."

Blood seeping up between my fingers.

Gasps for breath.

Last words...

I choke back a sob. Two men who meant so much to me. Two tragic deaths. Two sets of memories I never want to relive.

"There was nothing I could do but hold my hand over the wounds on his chest and pray."

Cutter snorts. "A lot of good praying did."

There are days I feel the same way. Being raised Catholic and spending my life in Catholic school and Catholic churches, religion was always a big part of everything. Saying the rosary every morning, going to Mass, communion, confession...but I haven't set foot in a church since Mario's death.

I would have for *Il Padrone's* funeral if it had been safe to attend. Missing it is more painful than I'd like to admit to myself. Holding on to something so intangible. Something I can't see and have to believe in with nothing more than blind faith. It goes against every logic-based, analytical thing I was taught as a cop. Yet, I can't bring myself to dismiss my belief in a higher power.

I gently drag my fingers over his scars. "I like to believe there's a reason for everything. Even though we may not be able to see it during our time on Earth."

Cutter turns on his side toward me. "You don't think that's naïve?"

I shrug. "Maybe."

"Well, here's what my many years in the military have taught me. If God does exist, he's a real fucking asshole."

The corner of my mouth quirks up. It's such a Cutter thing to say. "Saying something like that's going to send you to Hell."

He chuckles and flashes a lecherous grin. One of the rare glimpses of amusement he's exhibited in all this time we've spent together. "I've done a hell of a lot worse things that are gonna get me there, *principessa.*"

I lightly drag my nails across his chest, and he stills and shifts closer to me. His eyes glitter in the light but no longer with anger or frustration. That's been replaced with something that has heat pooling between my legs. I smile at him. "Like what you did to me on the boat earlier?"

A smirk tilts his lips. He rolls me onto my back and climbs on top of me, caging me in beneath him.

His hard cock presses between my legs. "Oh, *principessa.* That was nothing."

TWENTY-THREE

Cutter

M ilo's low growl wakes me from one of the deepest, peaceful sleeps I've had in a long time. No nightmares of beautiful, traitorous women.

I jerk up and glance down at where Milo lies near my left leg. At some point in the night, he shifted from sleeping near Valentina and moved back to his normal spot by me. But the growl is anything but normal. I can count the number of times he has made that sound in the last six years on one hand.

Something's wrong.

I listen and follow his line of vision to the window. We never pulled the drapes shut, and moonlight streams in, offering a hint of light in an otherwise dark room.

But nothing seems amiss.

The night is as silent as always, but I've learned the hard way that looks can be deceiving, or in this case, sounds. If Milo's reacting, something's happening that shouldn't be.

Valentina's soft, even breathing doesn't change. She didn't hear Milo. I shift over her and press my hand across her mouth. Her wide, terrified eyes fly open and meet mine.

"Shh." I hold my finger over my lips. I don't know what's

going on, but if someone is in or around the warehouse that shouldn't be, I'm not risking her making a sound. I lean down until my lips brush her ear. "Something's wrong. Take Milo and the Glock from the top drawer of my dresser and go wake Warwick and Grace. Stay up there with her. Lock yourselves in the bathroom until I give the all-clear."

She nods her understanding, and I release my hand from over her mouth. In less than ten seconds, she pulls on her tank top and yoga pants and has the gun in hand. I pull on a T-shirt and sweats and grab my Sig from the nightstand, and she scoops up Milo and approaches the door where I wait.

Preacher has this whole place and the area surrounding the warehouse rigged with cameras. If something is going on, he'll know, but until I know more, we have to assume the worst.

I turn the knob and ease the door open slowly. The darkness and silence of the warehouse are exactly as it should be at this hour. I motion for Valentina to stay back a moment, and she gives me a curt nod.

With silent steps against the cool concrete floor, I slip out the door, press my back to the wall, and scan the vast, dark space.

Fuck.

It's times like this, my limited vision really comes into play. But I know this building like the back of my fucking hand. The darkness is my friend and the enemy of anyone dumb enough to try to attack us here.

Like Arturo…

If it were any woman other than Valentina, I might worry about sending her to War's room alone. She'll be out in the open crossing the twenty or so feet from the door to my room over to the stairwell that will lead her up there. But I know that woman can take care of herself.

I turn back to the open the door to signal for her to go, and she steps forward and presses a harsh kiss to my lips before darting toward the stairs with Milo tucked under her left arm and my Glock ready in her right hand.

My lips tingle, and my heart thunders as she disappears into the darkness.

Don't worry. She's got this. I need to get to Preacher to see what's going on.

Even though his door is only a few feet to my left, it might as well be a mile while I'm this exposed. Though if anyone were in the warehouse and could see us, Valentina would have alerted them to my location and drawn fire already.

The ever-present, faint glow from the bank of monitors in Preacher's room shines from under the crack at the bottom of the door. I hurry down the hall, turn the knob, and slip inside.

Preacher doesn't even glance over at me. His entire focus is on the monitors in front of him.

I rush to him and lean over to examine the screens. "What's going on?"

"Motion alerts in the woods to the north a few minutes ago." He points to one of the monitors facing the north side of the property line. "We've got company."

Five armed figures dressed in black emerge from the tree line and advance toward the one major entry point of the warehouse.

Preacher's fingers fly across one of his keyboards. "Just sent texts to Rion, E, and Warwick." He finally glances up at me. "Where's Valentina?"

"I sent her to watch Grace and Milo up in War's room."

He nods. "Good. This could get ugly."

"No shit."

"The NODS are in the cabinet to your right. Third shelf from the top."

He knows what I need without me even asking. Unfortunately, most of our heavy weaponry is aboard the boats from the other day's raid, which sit right near the entrance our unexpected guests are about to penetrate. All we have are our pistols and a few tech toys Preacher keeps in here.

I grab my NODS goggles and slip them on, then shove three extra magazines for my Sig into my pockets. I glance over my shoulder at him as I take three more sets of NODS. "How many do you see? Just those five?"

He scans the monitors. "That's all I have right now."

"Got it. Keep us updated."

I slip out the door without another look back, carrying the goggles in my left hand with my Sig ready in the right. We've planned for an assault on the warehouse for years, even though we always hoped and prayed it would never come to this. Warwick and Preacher went to a lot of trouble to ensure this building and our vehicles weren't traceable back to any of us so the chances of someone finding us were slim.

But clearly not impossible.

Arturo.

My gut tells me this is him.

Who the fuck else would have the motive and be stupid enough to come at us on our home turf?

Rion and E make their way toward me in the dark hallway, bright figures in my artificially enhanced vision. I hand goggles to both of them and hold the final pair out for War. The secret technology doesn't merely help with my limited vision; it also enhances the ability to see the enemy for all the guys. A benefit we are sure to take advantage of when these fuckers are dumb enough enter our domain.

I signal for them to follow me, and we make our way to the end of the hallway near the stairwell. War's familiar figure appears near the base of the steps, but there's no other movement in the warehouse. No other signatures suggesting anyone has penetrated the interior.

Whoever these fuckers are, they haven't breached the door yet.

That gives us a few seconds to establish our positions to maximize our chances of success.

The boats would give us the best position and the ability to come at them from above, but they're too far away to make it to before those assholes enter, especially with E's bum leg. The sparseness of the main warehouse floor doesn't leave many options, but the massive wooden table in the center of the space will provide adequate cover, and the kitchen door is positioned perfectly to attack and also acts as a decent point of retreat if needed.

I motion for E to head to the kitchen and for Rion to follow me to the table. War will know to meet us there. They both nod their understanding before we split off and race through the eerily silent darkness.

Rion and I drop behind the table, and two seconds later, Warwick joins us. I hand him his NODS, and within a second, a loud blast from the direction of the entrance rocks the warehouse. Debris from the metal door flies and falls against the concrete. Smoke fills the air.

They've just announced their arrival.

How kind of them. And really fucking stupid.

The men advance into the warehouse through the smoke from the detonation. They don't stand a fucking chance. All three of us unleash on them, the advantage of our goggles making it as easy as fucking shooting fish in a barrel since they're lit up against the black backdrop of the cool air surrounding them.

Two of them immediately drop while the other three dive for anything they can find for cover. One makes it around *The Destiny*, and the other two move to the left of the door and drop behind a stack of boxes of supplies we had picked up earlier for our trip to Chicago tomorrow.

We duck back behind the table to reload.

Two down. Three to go.

Four against three. I like these odds.

Something metal clanks against the concrete to my right.

Shit.

There's no time to move before the flash-bang goes off. The blast of sound and light momentarily blinds me and likely Warwick and Rion and leaves my ears ringing, which is exactly what they wanted—to throw us off, even for a second.

Gunfire tears into the table, and bullets whizz past us and slam into the opposing wall. These guys mean business. It's too fucking bad they underestimated who they're dealing with.

I lean around the edge of the table and fire toward the two behind the boxes. Their fire ceases, but only for a second before their friend unleashes from *The Destiny*.

That motherfucker climbed aboard. Now he has the advantage of a higher vantage point. If we move from here, he'll peg us off one by one.

I didn't notice them wearing any night vision gear on the screen in Preacher's room, and they certainly don't have access to the technology we're using since Preacher "borrowed" it while he was still in good with the CIA, but they don't need top of the line anything to catch a glimpse of movement and shoot toward it.

That flash-bang illuminated enough for them to see where we are and get the layout of the warehouse. But if I can get to the base of the stairs, I can use them for cover and maybe sneak around to *The Destiny* from the blindside to take out the man up there. From that vantage point, I should be able to take out his two friends without much trouble.

I lean over to Rion. "You two cover me." I point toward the staircase and signal for them to watch me and follow. They all nod their agreement.

Go.

The cracks of their shots echo through the warehouse as I dart across the open area to the stairs. I press my back against the thick, metal joists of the stairs and glance across at Warwick and Rion to ensure they're okay. They unload their mags then drop back behind the table as another blast of bullets rains down on them from both the guys behind the boxes and the asshole on *The Destiny*.

None of them seemed to notice my movement. I duck under the stairs and pause before darting over the dock in front of *The Destiny*.

I slip between *The Destiny* and *The Calista* and climb the ladder up to *The Destiny's* deck. The volley of gunfire ceases, and I glance over the rail toward where the lone gunman up here was standing prior to me making my way over here.

He crouches, using the hull of the ship as cover—and leaving himself completely exposed to me coming from the other side. I fire off three shots. Two strike him dead center in the chest. The third hits him in the shoulder, but he clambers to his feet and ducks behind the pallet holding the cargo for Arturo.

Fuck.

They must be wearing vests.

Why can't anything just be fucking easy?

I could wait to see if he's dumb enough to make another move, but that hit to the shoulder hurt him. Chances are, he's bleeding badly and in a lot of pain, and hopefully, not thinking fast or clearly. Arturo's men have never been the brightest bulbs in the pack, so if this is his doing, we can only hope these guys aren't his top goons.

The only way to end this is to take a chance. I swing over the rail and drop into a crouch. He doesn't fire—either too scared to or incapable due to his wound. I dart over the opposite side of the pallet and peer around the corner. His weapon is on the deck, and his right hand is pressed over the wound on his left shoulder.

I reach out and press the barrel of my Sig to his temple. "Who sent you?"

TWENTY-FOUR

Valentina

S itting here on this cold, tile floor with a shaking Milo and quivering Grace while the guys are down there fighting God knows how many goons has my gut churning. Not being part of the action feels wrong. So fucking wrong.

Cazzo. Dovrei essere lì fuori.

I can help. A lot more so than playing babysitter to a scared dog and a pregnant woman.

They need another shooter, and there's no way any of the guys would let someone get near the damn staircase, let alone all the way up here without blowing off their head. Grace and Milo will be safe. And the guys will be safer with my help.

"What do you think is going on down there?" Grace's voice cracks, and she presses her hands to her belly.

For what seems like the hundredth time since I forced her in here a few minutes ago, I grab her hand and squeeze it reassuringly. "Those guys are badasses. I'm sure they're fine."

I wish I believed my own words, but the explosion that was likely the door being taken out and then the flash-bang means whoever is attacking the warehouse knows what they're doing. These aren't amateurs, which means the risk to the guys is genuine. Even the most incompetent of Arturo's men can get lucky with enough bullets.

My eyes drift down to the floor to the 9mm Warwick left with Grace. "You know how to use that thing, right?"

She narrows her annoyed, green gaze on me. "Of course, I do."

"Good. Stay here." I push to my feet and hand Milo to her.

The last thing we need is him darting out the door after me and out into the crossfire.

Grace wraps her arms around Milo with wide eyes. "Where are you going? Cutter told you to stay with me, didn't he?"

I scoff and roll my eyes. "Unlike some other people, I don't always do what Cutter tells me to."

And sometimes, that rebellion plays in my favor. It seems to turn him on as much as it infuriates him.

A tiny smile tugs at the corner of her lips despite the tension in the room. "You're good for him. You know that? He's been getting away with his bullshit for too long. But, please, be careful."

I shove to my feet, pull out the Glock Cutter gave me, and slowly ease open the bathroom door. I glance back at Grace. "Shoot anyone who touches this door if they don't announce themselves first."

She nods, and I slip out into the darkened bedroom. I make my way over to the row of windows that look down onto the warehouse floor. The thin paper that covers them is peeling up around the edges, offering me the perfect place to observe what's happening. I squat down and peer out through the tiny opening. All the lights are off in the warehouse, but moonlight streams in from where the door was blown off its hinges.

It's only faint light, but it's enough to see a portion of the warehouse.

Where is everyone?

Two bodies lie a few feet inside the door. I'd be worried except they're dressed in all black.

Every fiber of my being tells me to go out there to help the guys, but they know what they're doing. If I go, I may just get in the way.

A tiny flash of movement to the right of the entry door behind the boxes of supplies almost immediately draws gunfire from behind the table.

That's where the assholes must be hunkered down.

If Arturo sent them like my gut tells me, they know what they're doing, but they don't have the type of training and experience Cutter and Rion possess. They're nothing more than hired goons. They aren't trained soldiers. That should be to our advantage.

Gunfire erupts toward the boxes, but this time, from the direction of the boats. One of the guys must've moved over there at some point to get a better vantage point. Smart. It's an advantageous position. Of course, they would figure out a way to get up there.

Two bodies tumble out from behind the boxes.

Silence falls over the warehouse—an eerie silence that belies the bloodbath that happened down there. I wait for what feels like an hour and watch the bodies lying on the concrete floor.

What next?

Finally, a massive hulk of a human—who can only be Rion—shifts out from behind the table with his gun drawn. Warwick follows right behind him. They advance on the two who were just taken out, and Rion bends down to check them.

He must be satisfied they're dead because he turns back to Warwick and nods. "All clear!" His booming voice rings out in the warehouse, audible even up here through the glass in front of me.

E steps out from the kitchen and limps over to them.

I didn't even realize how hard I'd been clenching the gun in my hand until I release it and my fingers ache. I slowly open the door and make my way to the top of the stairs.

Where's Cutter?

A single floodlight flickers on at the center of the warehouse. Probably controlled by Preacher. It illuminates the fallout from the attack.

Bodies are strewn across the concrete floor.

Pieces of metal from the blown door scattered around.

Blood...

But...no Cutter.

My breath catches, I race down the stairs, frantically scanning the entire building I can see from here. Halfway down, *The Destiny* comes into view along with Cutter standing at the rail.

The coiled tension in my body releases almost instantly. I may have tried to convince myself I wasn't worried about him, but the pain in my chest from the lack of oxygen says otherwise.

Thank God.

He pulls off a pair of goggles covering his face, and his head turns toward me. His gaze meets mine, and I can't fight the sigh of relief that slips from my lips.

He's fine.

Cutter waves at the guys. "Get up here. I have one alive."

Warwick, Rion, and E wait for me to descend the rest of the stairs. They all hold the same goggles in their hands. It's quite the advantage, one they've clearly utilized tonight. The swift, sure way they decimated these men only solidifies my belief in how talented and lethal they are, especially when they work together as a team.

I reach out and take the goggles from Rion. "Are these night vision? Cutter had them on that night he was shot, but I never got to ask about them or examine them."

"Better than night vision. These are top-secret, military

tech. They also have thermal and all sorts of other capabilities. Preacher has a way of getting things we need."

I don't doubt it. Grace said he worked for the CIA doing computer forensics, cyber-warfare, offensive and defensive cybercollections. It's all high-tech computer stuff I can't even fathom. That kind of intelligence is impressive and terrifying all at the same time. And it means he has the connections to get just about anything on the down-low.

Preacher sticks out his head from the hallway. "I'm monitoring for any police radio traffic, but I doubt anyone's close enough to have heard anything."

Warwick nods and sets his NODS on the table. E and I add ours to the pile, and we all make our way over to *The Destiny*. I climb up the ladder, followed by Warwick, Rion, and a much slower E.

Cutter waits for us on the deck. A pool of blood spills out from behind one of the pallets. He nods down, and I approach with the guys behind me.

A man dressed in all black sits propped against the pallet. His right hand pressed over a wound in his shoulder doesn't seem to be doing much to stem the flow of blood.

Warwick glances at the man and then looks to Cutter. "Did you question him yet?"

Cutter shakes his head. "Just asked who sent him."

"And?"

Cutter shrugs. "And he didn't want to cooperate. I figured it would be better to do this together."

The man sneers at Cutter then spits. A glob of phlegm and blood lands on Cutter's bare foot.

Oh, merda...

Cutter glances down at it, then gives him the cold, emotionless smirk that spells trouble. The man has no idea what he's in for. Cutter crouches in front of him. "We can do this the easy way or the hard way. This..." he pushes the barrel of his gun into the man's temple, "is the easy way.

The hard way takes much longer and is far more painful for you."

He reaches up with his free hand, knocks the man's hand from the wound, and digs his thumb into it. The man screams and thrashes, trying to knock Cutter's hand away, but Cutter holds firm and twists his thumb even deeper.

He leans in closer to the man. "Who sent you?"

As I expected, this isn't some superior soldier well-trained on how to survive an interrogation from a trained operative. This guy is nothing more than muscle.

Through clenched teeth, the goon manages to answer. "I can't…he'll kill me."

Rion barks out a laugh and moves to stand behind Cutter, his massive frame surely even more intimidating when you're staring up at it, prone and bleeding. "You're dead either way, friend. Might as well make this easy on yourself and confirm what we already know."

Tense silence fills the air, the only sound the man's heavy breathing and the occasional drip of blood onto the deck. His eyes dart from Rion to Cutter to Warwick to his right and E leaning against the rail to his left. They finally land on me.

Do I know him? Does he know me?

There isn't any flash of recognition when his eyes meet mine, only an unspoken plea for help as if he thinks that because I'm a woman, I'm somehow weak and emotional enough to do what I can to save his life.

He's an even bigger *cretino* than I thought. "You better answer their question."

His cold eyes widen slightly. Maybe he finally realizes how serious they are. He coughs, a rattling sound filled with a tell-tale liquid gurgle that means there's blood in his lungs. "Arturo."

It's not a surprise. It also answers the question of whether the *Marcella Marie* was a set-up. After he didn't hear from the crew, he must have decided to take the guys out another way.

And now that he knows I'm here with them, he thought he could take us all out tonight and take the heroin, instead of doing it tomorrow in Chicago, where we would be on *his* property and there are far more prying eyes and potentials to get caught.

Cutter issues a low growl. The confirmation that it's Arturo only enflames the already burning hatred he has for that man. "How did you find the warehouse?"

Arturo's hitman shakes his head. "I don't know. He gave us the address."

Merda.

Probably the same way I did. If Arturo somehow managed to find my hotel room, they would have seen Milo's tag. With the resources available to the Marconis, locating this place wouldn't have been difficult once they had that tiny piece of information—Cutter's name. Arturo may not have known what it meant, but he knows Warwick and the crew operate out of this area. So once he got an address, he had to have put two and two together.

But…this might not be a bad thing.

I step forward, closer to the man who just tried to kill us. "Cutter?"

Cutter shifts his gaze to meet mine but doesn't move away from the captive.

"Take your thumb out of that man's shoulder. I think I know how we can get to Arturo."

TWENTY-FIVE

Cutter

The massive metal gates at the rear of *Il Padrone's* property swing open with a heavy creak. A light drizzle falls, and a dense fog settles over the area. Despite it being almost three in the morning, the huge mansion at the top of the small hill still has lights shining in a few windows.

Arturo is awake...and waiting.

Gravel crunches under the tires of the black SUV as I drive it along the narrow driveaway up the hill and park at the rear of the house. The vehicle the attack squad came in was parked in the woods a few miles from the warehouse, and it was exactly what we needed to carry out Valentina's plan.

I glance over my shoulder to where Warwick, Rion, and Valentina sit behind me, all dressed in black and armed to the teeth. Ready for fucking action.

This plan of hers is actually pretty brilliant. After forcing our captive to make the call to Arturo, confirming the success of their mission, he won't be anticipating anything, especially us. And with her knowledge of the inner workings of the property and the security system, we'll be able to get in and get to him before the remaining guards know what's happening.

The first step was making it onto the property, and the gate opener in the SUV made that easy as fuck. Now, we just need to get into the house and to Arturo's office, the place where *Il Padrone* used to conduct business.

Valentina's gaze meets mine, and she nods. "Time to go. I'll go in first. Follow me straight into the surveillance room. Once we take out the man there, the rest will be easy."

Famous last words.

Things almost never go as planned, but if we do take out Arturo, any hiccups along the road will be worth it.

I nod my agreement, but something twists my gut. Something unfamiliar.

Maybe it's the thought of Valentina being the first one in, the first one exposed to any gunfire that's bringing it on.

The first in is usually the one in the most danger.

Trust her.

I have to let her go. She's the only one who can. And she's not some wilting flower. She's proven her skill with a weapon and her willingness to do whatever it takes to end this. To end the Marconis once and for all.

She throws open the door and slides out of the SUV. Rion and Warwick file out after Valentina, and I follow behind their approach to the house with our faces carefully turned away from the cameras. Unless the guy manning the surveillance room looks closely, he won't be able to tell we aren't the team returning, and no one will be expecting anything amiss.

Valentina pauses at the door and unlocks it with the key off the keychain we took from our final "guest" before I shot him in the head. There was no further use for him, and he probably would have bled to death anyway. I promised to take it easy on him if he answered our questions, but as much as I wanted to play and have some fun, time was of the essence.

The darkened hallway gives us plenty of shadows with which to conceal our movements while making our way toward the surveillance room. At the third door on the right,

Valentina pauses. She nods to the door, turns the knob, and pushes it open.

A single guy sits inside, staring at a bank of monitors. He turns back to greet us, not knowing it's the final moment of his life.

Sorry, asshole. You picked the wrong side.

Valentina fires a single shot that hits him in the center of the chest, and he topples from his chair and onto the plush carpet beneath.

That shouldn't be so fucking hot, but watching her work with such precision has my cock hardening.

She is one badass woman.

Completely different from anyone I've met before or probably ever will. It almost makes me regret that she'll be leaving once we take care of Arturo. But this isn't her home. Italy is. She had a life and a career there. Family. Friends. Maybe even someone who was more than a friend before she came here.

She points to the bank of monitors. "I know Warwick has been here before, but for the rest of you, the office is here." She points to a closed door on a monitor. "Down the hallway to the left. Second door. There's no camera in there, but Arturo will have at least two men with him or close, either outside or in the room." She scans the screens and points. "This is the hall that leads back to the office, and I don't see anyone there."

Too easy.

Warwick sighs. "Does this seem a little too easy for anyone?"

I nod. "Exactly what I was just thinking."

She shakes her head. "No. He just thinks he's safe now. Trust me on this. I know him. He doesn't believe there is any possible way someone could get in here, and since he thinks we're all dead, he's let down his guard."

I hope she's right.

This needs to end. The Marconis have been fucking with us long enough.

I squeeze Valentina's shoulder. "Come on, let's go do this."

It may spell the end for whatever this thing is between Valentina and me, but it will also mean the end of the Marconis.

She sucks in a breath, nods, and she follows me out of the room with Warwick and Rion bringing up the rear. We make our way down the hallway toward the office and pause outside the closed door. No sign of the men who should be guarding Arturo. They must be inside with him.

Here we fucking go.

This has been a long time coming. Arturo needs to get what he deserves.

I hold up my hand, ensure all eyes are on me, and motion for them to follow. This is the moment we've been waiting for, our chance to finally end our servitude to this fucking prick. I push open the door and step in with my gun pointed. Valentina and the guys are only a second behind me.

Arturo jerks his head up from something he was looking at on his desk, his dark eyes go wide, and the two men leaning against the wall lurch to their feet and reach for their guns.

I shake my head. "I wouldn't do that if I were you."

With four guns pointed at them and their boss, they think better of it.

Arturo's eyes narrow on me, then flick to Warwick, then Rion, and finally come to a stop on Valentina. "I should've known you weren't gone. When my men reported back from the hotel that they couldn't locate you, they said you must have left town. But I had a gut feeling you were still around. I just never anticipated you'd be slumming it with these guys. Then I get the call from them, offering you and the heroin in exchange for a release from their debt, and I figured you were being held captive. It appears I was mistaken. Are you fucking one of these thugs?"

I can't help it. The growl rumbles low in my chest, and I take a step toward the desk, leveling my gun on his chest.

A smirk crosses Arturo's lips. "This one?" He raises an eyebrow at me and scans me from head to foot. His gaze flicks back to Valentina. "I didn't realize you had a thing for damaged goods."

Even with my aviators on, I can't fully conceal the scars, and I make no attempt to hide my anger at his comment. I shift the barrel of my gun between his eyes.

"Fuck you, Arturo." Valentina snarls at him. "You're over. *This* is over."

He chuckles, low and dark. "Is it? Why? Because you said so? Because *you* want it to be?" His lip curls up. "What did you think was going to happen when you came in here? I was just going to roll over and turn over my empire to you just because you have the old man's blood coursing through your veins?"

Valentina freezes next to me.

What the...? Did he just say the old man's blood?

I turn my focus to her and wait for her to explain. He can't mean what I think he does. It's impossible. She couldn't have hidden this, couldn't have kept this from us. Preacher would have found something. There would have been *some* evidence of her paternity somewhere in the thousands of sources he searched to find out her background.

And more importantly, she wouldn't have kept this from us...from *me*. Not after what we did together, after what I told her, after what happened between us.

She wouldn't.

But...she did. The smug look on Arturo's face and the fear in her amber eyes confirms it.

Arturo's gaze flicks between us, and a smile twists his lips. "Oh. I see. They don't know."

Her gun doesn't waver as she points it at him, but she glances at me quickly before returning her focus to Arturo. "I wasn't even sure you knew."

He nods slowly and leans back in his chair casually, like there aren't four people waiting to kill him, standing right in front of him. Like he didn't just reveal one big fucking plot twist in this epic family tale of betrayal. "I wasn't sure. But I had my suspicion when he brought you on that there was something more happening. I thought maybe you were fucking the old man, but after watching the way he interacted with you, it was clearly more of a father-daughter relationship."

"Father...*daughter*?" I look to Valentina, but she avoids my gaze, keeping her focus on Arturo.

She can't even look at me. The woman fucking lied to me and betrayed us.

Who is the enemy in this room now?

Arturo smirks. "Is that why *Il Padrone* brought you here? To take me out so that you could step up to your rightful place at the head of the family?"

Rightful place? You've got to be shitting me!

A strange heat climbs up the back of my neck as the reality of it all creeps in.

She's *Il Padrone's* daughter.

Arturo's cousin.

She's a fucking *liar*.

The woman who was in my bed and in my arms only a few hours ago shakes her head and frantically looks from me to her *cousin*. "It doesn't matter why he brought me here. What matters is, your services as head of the Marconi family are no longer needed."

He chuckles and rises to his feet, holding out his hands, palms up. "As if you have the balls to do anything about it. You're just—"

Bang. Bang. Bang. Bang. Bang. Bang. Bang.

She unloads on him, emptying the entire magazine straight into his chest. The man who assassinated his own uncle to take over the business only a week ago lunges forward and grabs the desk for a moment before he topples onto the rug.

Deafening silence fills the room.

She slowly lowers her gun and looks to the two men standing on either side of the desk. "You have two choices. You're either with me or against me."

Neither takes long to consider their options. They look at each other and then both nod at Valentina. "We're with you."

Mindless goons. They watched her gun down their boss in cold fucking blood, and now, they're at her beck and call. It's so easy for them to switch sides.

And apparently, it's just as easy for the woman I had started to trust.

I've experienced significant pain in my life, but the sting of betrayal has to be the harshest and most intense.

How the fuck could she?

Valentina turns to her two new henchmen. "Good. Remove his body and call everyone to the house. We need to have a family meeting."

TWENTY-SIX

Valentina

I make my way around the desk that Father sat behind for so many years, running his empire. It was his sanctuary. The one place he felt safe from Arturo, even at the end. Where we sat together and made plans, plans for me to take over my birthright.

The bloodstain left on the floor from Arturo's body only gets a passing glance. He is the past, nothing more than a dark blip on the timeline of the Marconi empire.

I am the future of this family.

My family.

Rather than replace the rug, it's going to stay as a reminder of what happens to someone who betrays a Marconi. There is no forgiveness, no second chances, no ability to walk away.

I lower myself into the plush leather chair behind the desk and finally face Warwick, Rion, and Cutter. Their stunned expressions aren't really a surprise given what just happened. Neither is the anger radiating off all three of them.

It has to be a shock.

If the situation were reversed, I would feel the same way.

Betrayed. It's why keeping it from them, from Cutter especially, weighed so heavily on me.

I recline in the chair and raise my hands in question with a smile. "So?"

Cutter shoves his gun into the holster and finally manages to speak. "You fucking used us. The same way your father used you."

That stings a little.

A lot, actually.

I offer a slight shrug.

He's not wrong, but I don't think the situations are the same at all.

"The situations are quite different, Cutter. My father used me to take out his competition to secure a stronger hold on his dealings in Italy. You would've killed Arturo anyway, regardless of whether I was involved with your team or not. I didn't use you to do anything you wouldn't have done anyway."

I glance around the office Arturo has already made such major changes to. The photographs of *Il Padrone* with various celebrities and government officials and friends that once lined the walls have been replaced with ones of my deceitful cousin. It turns my stomach the way he moved in here without any regard for the man he usurped.

Bastardo.

Those atrocities need to be removed. I climb from the chair and walk over to the wall. Arturo's smiling face stares back at me. I pull it down, then make my way to the next. One by one, I drop them into the wastebasket while the guys remain silent behind me.

No one is saying anything. Whether they want me to continue or not, I owe them an explanation. They did, after all, make this all possible.

I sigh as I toss another picture into the trashcan. "You see, my father had a plan when he called me over from Italy. He had been noticing some troublesome behavior from my cousin and had begun questioning his original plan to leave Arturo in charge of the family." I wander over to the far wall and remove another set of photos from there. They join the others. "He knew I would never betray him, even though I didn't know who he was."

Warwick holds up his hands and shakes his head in disbelief. "Whoa, whoa, whoa, you didn't know he was your father?"

It's hard to believe, but maybe once I explain, they'll understand. "No. I grew up in a very small town. My mother had always told me my father died before I was born. That was the accepted story. But there was a man who came to visit us once or twice a year. I knew him as Uncle Galasso. He and my mother continued their affair in secret. His late wife never knew, and he never had any children with her, which is why Arturo was the presumed heir. But when all this went down and I arrived in America, he told me everything and that he had made a decision that he needed to remove Arturo permanently and put me in his place at the head of the family when he decided to retire."

Rion's brow furrows, and he crosses his massive arms over his chest. "Not to sound like an asshole here, but women aren't allowed to be heads of the family."

Antiquated nonsense.

I return to my chair and sit. "Why not? What about Rosetta Cutolo or Grisela Blanco in Colombia? They both ran massive criminal empires worth billions of dollars for years. They were more ruthless than some of the men who ran the cartels."

Warwick nods. "You're right."

I flash him a tiny smile. "I know. *Il Padrone* had hoped we could gather enough evidence against Arturo that when he had him taken out, there wouldn't be any backlash from anyone in the organization about my stepping in. He thought by the time I would have to step up, he would have paved my way and showed me the ropes and put me in a position to be respected by his men. We never anticipated that Arturo would go so far so fast."

Cutter releases the jaw he's had clenched the last few minutes. "And you didn't think this might be important fucking information for us to have from the very beginning?"

I knew he would be the hardest to convince and the least accepting of the truth. I just hadn't anticipated how hard it would be to look at him when I told him. "Would you have helped me if you knew I planned to take over as head of the family?"

The silence from all three of them is the only answer I need.

"Exactly. You planned to take out the Marconis to remove any debt you have with the family and to get out from under their control. If I had told you that assisting me in taking out Arturo would only put *me* at the head of the family you hoped to eliminate, you might've killed me just as easily as you did him."

The flush of anger that crosses Cutter's cheeks tells me I'm right. He wouldn't have hesitated to kill me in the beginning if he knew who I was. Their vendetta was against the entire family. It wouldn't have mattered that I didn't know I was a member until recently, or that I wished them no ill-will.

He stares me down from behind those damn glasses and silence fills the room, the tension mounting with every second that passes. Then he turns slowly, clears his throat, and looks to Warwick and Rion. "Guys, I need to talk to Valentina." He glances over at me. "Or is it Miss Marconi now?"

Warwick shakes his head. "I don't think that's a good idea, Cutter. You're pretty angry and—"

"Get the *fuck* out!" Cutter's words vibrate through my

bones, and Warwick and Rion both hold up their hands in surrender as they move toward the door.

Rion tosses me an apologetic look. "Okay, man, but just don't do anything stupid."

Cutter's not a stupid man, but anyone is capable of anything when they feel betrayed. Right now, Cutter's most definitely feeling betrayed.

I'm so sorry.

I wish there had been another way, but I didn't have a choice if I wanted to stay alive.

Cutter follows Warwick and Rion to the door, closes it behind them, and turns the lock. He stands, facing the door for a few seconds. His back rises and falls with his heaving breaths.

The desire to go to him, to wrap my arms around him and apologize, to offer him comfort, is so strong, I start to rise, but he turns back to me. His approach to the desk is slow and deliberate. He flattens his palms on the wooden top and leans across it slightly to stare me down through those damn glasses.

I'm so sick of looking back at my reflection when all I really want to see is him. "Why do you look so angry, Cutter?"

"Why do I look so angry? Why do I look so fucking angry? Are you kidding me right now, *principessa?* Perhaps I should have kept calling you *little mouse* because you're sneaky as fuck."

"That's not fair, Cutter—"

He scoffs and shakes his head. "I had a dream, you know. Right after you arrived at the warehouse. A dream that was a warning. That you were not what you appeared. You were a wolf in sheep's clothing, as they say. I should've listened to my fucking gut."

I release a sigh and watch him for a moment. The cord of muscle along the side of his neck bulges, and a tiny vein in his forehead throbs. I can't blame him for his anger because he's clearly not understanding. "Cutter...this is a *good* thing. Why can't you see that?"

"How is this a good thing? That you were able to lie to us repeatedly? That you will be able to get us to do your fucking dirty work without a second thought?"

Maledizione!

He's so worked up over what I didn't tell him that he doesn't see the bigger picture here. "You're free. All of you are free from your debt to *Il Padrone* and Arturo. I'm not going to make you pay back another dime. If you choose to continue to do the work you have been doing for my family, you will do it of your own free will. Jobs you want to do, not because I order you to do them."

He continues to stare me down, with no apparent abatement in his anger level.

I'm losing him.

"Don't let your anger cloud your judgment here, Cutter."

He scoffs, anger tightening the cord on his neck. "And you're just gonna let us walk away that easily? You're just gonna give up the hundreds of thousands of dollars of debt and our capabilities you desperately need to keep this business running just like that?"

I nod slowly. "Just. Like. That."

He shoves off the desk and storms around the massive piece of furniture toward me. I swivel my chair to face him, and he steps between my legs and reaches down and wraps his hand around my throat and uses it to drag me to my feet.

In any other circumstances, this action against the head of the family would've seen him dead in two seconds flat. But this is Cutter, and he needs to do and say what he needs to do and say to let this go.

His hand tightens on my throat, and he leans in until our lips almost touch. "You expect me to fucking believe you're going to let us walk away? That you didn't have some ulterior motive from day one when you hooked up with me? That you weren't looking for a way to get in with us by getting into my bed?"

I reach up and pull off his glasses and set them on the desk next to us. "These damn things are clouding your judgment again."

One icy-blue eye and one milky-white one stare back at me. "You have no fucking right." His hand tightens again.

Heat spreads through my limbs, and moisture floods between my legs. "I have every fucking right, Cutter. I've more than earned that right and my spot behind his desk. You know me. You may be questioning that right now because of what you just learned, but you know me. And I know you. And this," I point to the chair behind me, "is good for all of us."

"Oh? You think so, *principessa?*" He kicks the chair out of the way and pushes me backward until I hit the wall behind us. His free hand flattens against it, caging me in. "Or do I have to call you *regina* now that you've taken your throne?"

He had no idea how accurate he was calling me *principessa* this whole time, but I don't need to be called queen.

A smile tugs at my lips despite the continued anger he's displaying. With Cutter, anger is the same thing as affection. He doesn't get angry if he doesn't care. That's something I've learned to accept very quickly, no matter how difficult it might be.

It's just part of what makes him Cutter.

He growls low and dark. "Maybe I need to do something to wipe that damn smirk off your face."

I reach up and capture his face between my palms. "There's no need, *amore mio.* I already know your favorite kind of torture, and I'm not sure I can withstand it again."

He flexes his palm again and brushes his thumb over my pulse. I've never wanted him to fuck me so much as I do in this moment. Arguing with Cutter is tantamount to foreplay, and it gets me hotter than anything ever has in my entire life.

He brushes his lips against mine. "Don't think for a

fucking second that residing in this house and sitting in that chair means you're the boss here."

I bury my fingers in his hair and nod against his hold. "Don't worry, *amore mio.* I wouldn't dream of it."

Epilogue

CUTTER

ONE MONTH LATER

"Cutter!" Preacher's muffled voice floats through the door but coupled with the incessant pounding against the wood, he's made it crystal clear that whatever it is he wants is urgent.

Valentina clenches her pussy around my cock and grabs my face, turning it back to look at her instead of the door. She presses her heels into my lower back and narrows her eyes. "Don't you even *think* about stopping."

"Fuck, *principessa*! Keep doing that, and this will be over soon anyway."

I roll my hips, pull back, and drive into her, deep and hard. She moans and drops her hands to my back, digging her nails into the skin there, and probably leaving those marks I love seeing so goddamn much in the mirror when I look the morning after.

Her mark.

Her claim.

Bam. Bam. Bam.

"Cutter!" Preacher pounds again.

Bam. Bam. Bam.

Each slam of his fist coincides with a thrust of my hips. It sends the tempo racing.

I turn my face toward the door to ensure he can hear me. "Jesus Christ, Preacher. Five fucking minutes!"

If I even last that long...

The way Valentina undulates beneath me, there's a good chance I won't.

He mumbles something angry and unintelligible, but the pounding on the door stops.

Valentina raises an eyebrow at me, an annoyed twist to her lips. "Five minutes?"

I roll onto my back, bringing her with me to straddle my hips. Her perfect breasts sway as she slides up my cock, then slowly sinks back down, squeezing the whole way.

Fuck yes.

I press my thumb to her clit and swirl it in the way I know will send her flying. "We won't need that long with as close as you've got me."

She groans, then smirks and rolls her hips as she grinds down and clenches my cock like a vise. "This is why I prefer your coming to see me in Chicago, *amore mio*. No interruptions."

True. Her place is far nicer, and the security there means there are never any interruptions, but splitting our time between homes is still necessary as long as we're working for the Marconis and I need to plan with the boys.

I dig my fingers into her hips and shove up into her, meeting her glide down. "Shut up and fuck me, *principessa*."

She plants her hands against my shoulders and leans down to press a kiss to my eager mouth. Her dark hair falls around us like curtains shutting out the world.

All that exists is the two of us.

The feel of her wet cunt wrapped around my cock.

Her tongue sliding across my lips.

My thumb covered in her arousal, slowly working her up to the orgasm we're both chasing.

I dig my heels into the mattress and thrust up to meet her movements. She pulls her lips from mine. Her breathing hitches. The low burn of my impending orgasm starts at the base of my spine.

"Come on, *principessa*."

She mewls and throws back her head. I pinch her clit between my thumb and forefinger, and she bucks forward and cries out, her rhythm faltering. I hold her in place with my left hand and drive up into her. Her pussy milks my cock, and two more thrusts is all it takes for me to fall over that edge with her.

With a sigh, she collapses on me and buries her face against my neck. Warm breath flutters across my damp skin, and I drag my fingers down her spine. She shudders and presses her mouth behind my ear.

"Are you two done fucking yet?"

Oh, you've got to be fucking kidding me.

Valentina rolls off me, and I rise to my feet and storm over to the door. I throw it open, not giving a single fuck that I'm naked.

Preacher doesn't even react to my nudity. "About fucking time. We have a serious problem."

He glances over my shoulder toward the bed.

I shift along with him to block his view. "What the hell, man? You have a fucking death wish?"

It's been a while since Preacher's gotten laid, but checking out Valentina is a major violation of the bro-code.

He raises his hands in surrender. "Nah, dude. But you better bring her along. This affects her, too."

Well, shit.

I hope you enjoyed reading *Rogue Wave*, the second book in The Inland Seas Series. The third book, *Safe Harbor*, is available at all retailers.

PREACHER
When it comes to firewalls, no one
gets through my defenses.
For the past five years, protecting this band of f-ed up brothers
has been my mission.
But Everly pulls me from my cave and does the
one thing no one else ever has...
She makes me believe there's a life outside
the world on my screens.
Too bad actions have consequences, ones that threaten
everything and everyone around me.
Including the beautiful tattoo artist who has managed to etch
herself onto my heart.

EVERLY
The emotional upheaval of the last six months would be
enough to break anyone.
And I can already feel myself cracking.
A tall, sexy, tattooed bad boy is the last thing
I need thrown into the mix.
All I want is to keep my head down and pour
my pain into my art.
But Preacher walks into my life and offers me safety in a world
where I thought there was none.
Until our pasts finally catch up with us...

Preacher and Everly.
Fear and loss.

Hope and heartbreak.
This harbor may be their salvation.

AVAILABLE NOW: books2read.com/SafeHarbor
Sign up for Gwyn's newsletter to stay up to date on releases and other news: www.gwynmcnamee.com/newsletter

About the Author

Gwyn McNamee is an attorney, writer, wife, and mother (to one human baby and two fur babies). Originally from the Midwest, Gwyn relocated to her husband's home town of Las Vegas in 2015 and is enjoying her respite from the cold and snow. Gwyn has been writing down her crazy stories and ideas for years and finally decided to share them with the world. She loves to write stories with a bit of suspense and action mingled with romance and heat.

When she isn't either writing or voraciously devouring any books she can get her hands on, Gwyn is busy adding to her tattoo collection, golfing, and stirring up trouble with her perfect mix of sweetness and sarcasm (usually while wearing heels).

Gwyn loves to hear from her readers.
Here is where you can find her:
Facebook:
https://www.facebook.com/AuthorGwynMcNamee/
Twitter:
https://twitter.com/GwynMcNamee
Instagram:
https://www.instagram.com/gwynmcnamee
Bookbub:
https://www.bookbub.com/authors/gwyn-mcnamee
FB Reader Group:

https://www.facebook.com/groups/1667380963540655/
Website:
https://www.gwynmcnamee.com

OTHER WORKS BY GWYN MCNAMEE

The Inland Seas Series (Romantic Suspense)

Squall Line (Book One)

WAR

Out on the water, I'm in control.

I don't make mistakes.

But the fiery redhead destroyed my plans and

left me no choice.

I had to take her.

Now I'm fighting for my life while battling my growing attraction for my hostage.

Grace may have started my downfall, but she could also be my salvation.

GRACE

The moment he stepped foot on my ship, I knew he was trouble.

He took me, and now, my life is in his hands.

But things aren't what they seem, and Warwick isn't

who he appears.

The man who holds me hostage is slowly working his way into my heart even as greater dangers loom on the horizon.

War and Grace.

Dark and light.

Love and hate.

This storm may destroy them both...

Rogue Wave (Book Two)

CUTTER

Complete the mission.

It's what I was trained to do—no matter what.

But when things go to shit right in front of me, my objective gets compromised by a set of fathomless amber eyes.

This isn't a woman's world.

Yet, Valentina refuses to see how dangerous the course she's plotted really is.

How dangerous I am.

VALENTINA

The man who saved my life is just as lethal as the one trying to take it.

Maybe even more.

While he may have rescued me, in the end,

Cutter is my enemy.

The one intent on destroying everything I've striven for.

But the scars of his past draw me closer even though I know I should move away.

Cutter and Valentina.

Anger and desire.

Fight and surrender.

This wave may drag them both under…

AVAILABLE AT ALL RETAILERS:

books2read.com/RogueWave

Safe Harbor (Book Three)

PREACHER

When it comes to firewalls, no one gets

through my defenses.

For the past five years, protecting this band of f-ed up brothers has
been my mission.

But Everly pulls me from my cave and does the one thing no one
else ever has...

She makes me believe there's a life outside the world

on my screens.

Too bad actions have consequences, ones that threaten everything
and everyone around me.

Including the beautiful tattoo artist who has managed to etch herself
onto my heart.

EVERLY

The emotional upheaval of the last six months would be enough to
break anyone.

And I can already feel myself cracking.

A tall, sexy, tattooed bad boy is the last thing I need thrown into
the mix.

All I want is to keep my head down and pour my pain

into my art.

But Preacher walks into my life and offers me safety in a world
where I thought there was none.

Until our pasts finally catch up with us…

Preacher and Everly.

Fear and loss.

Hope and heartbreak.

This harbor may be their salvation.

AVAILABLE AT ALL RETAILERS:

books2read.com/SafeHarbor

Anchor Point (Book Four)

ELIJAH

Life outside the walls of my prison cell is far harder than the time I
did inside.

There, I had my misery to keep me company.

Out here, I'm forced to face the reality of

everything I've lost.

Nothing can repair the gaping hole in my chest.

Yet, a broken woman wrapped in chains threatens to unravel the
tangle of excuses I use to keep everyone

at arm's length.

But letting Evangeline into my world means exposing her to the real
threat.

Me.

And all the terrible things that come along with that.

EVANGELINE

Taken.

Enslaved.

To be sold to the highest bidder.

The monsters who stole me away from my life

have no conscience.

I'm not so sure the man who rescues me is any different.

He's an ex-con and a pirate— not to be trusted.

But the dark veil of anguish that shrouds him can't hide the truth of who he is at his core.

Elijah isn't the enemy.

He may be broken and tormented…

And exactly what I need.

Elijah and Evangeline.

Agony and regret.

Faith and acceptance.

This anchor may pull them both down…

AVAILABLE AT ALL RETAILERS:

books2read.com/AnchorPoint

Dark Tide (Book Five)

RION

There is no black and white in this life.

The line between right and wrong blurs.

I'm constantly crossing it.

Saving a life is just as easy as taking one.

And I'm damn good at both.

Finding a woman who can survive in this world was never on the radar.

But Gabriella pulls me from the bottom of a bottle and touches me in a way no one else can.

Too bad secrets and lies have a way of catching up with everyone.

GABRIELLA

How did I end up here, slinging drinks at a dive bar in the middle of nowhere?

The choices that brought me to this were never even a glimmer of possibility only a few years ago.

How things can change so fast...

And now, my path puts me on a collision course

with Orion Gates.

His bigger-than-life size and personality should

be a warning.

The profession he's chosen should be the ultimate

final straw.

But instead, I find myself unable to resist his pull.

A decision that could lead to the end of all of us.

Rion and Gabriella.

Lust and lies.

Betrayal and ruin.

This tide may drown everyone...

AVAILABLE AT ALL RETAILERS:

books2read.com/DarkTide

The Hawke Family Series

Savage Collision **(The Hawke Family - Book One)**

He's everything she didn't know she wanted. She's everything he thought he could never have.

The last thing I expect when I walk into The Hawkeye Club is to fall head over heels in lust. It's supposed to be a rescue mission. I have to get my baby sister off the pole, into some clothes, and out of the grasp of the pussy peddler who somehow manipulated her into stripping. But the moment I see Savage Hawke and verbally spar with him, my ability to remain rational flies out the window and my libido takes center stage. I've never wanted a relationship—my time is better spent focusing on taking down the scum running this city— but what I want and what I need are apparently two different things.

Danika Eriksson storms into my office in her high heels and on her high horse. Her holier-than-thou attitude and accusations should offend me, but instead, I can't get her out of my head or my heart. Her incomparable drive, take-no prisoners attitude, and blatant honesty captivate me and hold me prisoner. I should steer clear, but my self-preservation instinct is apparently dead—which is exactly what our relationship will be once she knows everything. It's only a matter of time.

The truth doesn't always set you free. Sometimes, it just royally screws you.

AVAILABLE AT ALL RETAILERS:

books2read.com/SavageCollision

Tortured Skye (The Hawke Family - Book Two)

She's always been off-limits. He's always just out of reach.

Falling in love with Gabe Anderson was as easy as breathing. Fighting my feelings for my brother's best friend was agonizingly hard. I never imagined giving in to my desire for him would cause such a destructive ripple effect. That kiss was my grasp at a lifeline —something, anything to hold me steady in my crumbling life. Now,

I have to suffer with the fallout while trying to convince him it's all worth the consequences.

Guilt overwhelms me—over what I've done, the lives I've taken, and more than anything, over my feelings for Skye Hawke. Craving my best friend's little sister is insanely self-destructive. It never should have happened, but since the moment she kissed me, I haven't been able to get her out of my mind. If I take what I want, I risk losing everything. If I don't, I'll lose her and a piece of myself. The raging storm threatening to rain down on the city is nothing compared to the one that will come from my decision.

Love can be torture, but sometimes, love is the only thing that can save you.

AVAILABLE AT ALL RETAILERS:

Books2read.com/Tortured-Skye

Stone Sober (**The Hawke Family - Book Three**)

She's innocent and sweet. He's dark and depraved.

Stone Hawke is precisely the kind of man women are warned about — handsome, intelligent, arrogant, and intricately entangled with some dangerous people. I should stay away, but he manages to strip my soul bare with just a look and dominates my thoughts. Bad decisions are in my past. My life is (mostly) on track, even if it is no longer the one to medical school. I can't allow myself to cave to the fierce pull and ardent attraction I feel toward the youngest Hawke.

Nora Eriksson is off-limits, and not just because she's my brother's employee and sister-in-law. Despite the fact she's stripping at The Hawkeye Club, she has an innocent and pure heart. Normally, the only thing that appeals to me about innocence is the opportunity to taint it. But not when it comes to Nora. I can't expose her to the filth permeating my life. There are too many things I can't control, things completely out of my hands. She doesn't deserve any of it, but the power she holds over me is stronger than any addiction.

The hardest battles we fight are often with ourselves, but only through defeating our own demons can we find true peace.

AVAILABLE AT ALL RETAILERS:

books2read.com/StoneSober

Building Storm (The Hawke Family - Book Four)

She hasn't been living. He's looking for a way to forget it all.

My life went up in flames. All I'm left with is my daughter and ashes. The simple act of breathing is so excruciating, there are days I wish I could stop altogether. So I have no business being at the party, and I definitely shouldn't be in the arms of the handsome stranger. When his lips meet mine, he breathes life into me for the first time since the day the inferno disintegrated my world. But loving again isn't in the cards, and there are even greater dangers to face than trying to keep Landon McCabe out of my heart.

Running is my only option. I have to get away from Chicago and the betrayal that shattered my world. I need a new life-one without attachments. The vibrancy of New Orleans convinces me it's possible to start over. Yet in all the excitement of a new city, it's Storm Hawke's dark, sad beauty that draws me in. She isn't looking for love, and we both need a hot, sweaty release without feelings getting involved. But even the best laid plans fail, and life can leave you burned.

Love can build, and love can destroy. But in the end, love is what raises you from the ashes.

AVAILABLE AT ALL RETAILERS:

books2read.com/BuildingStorm

Tainted Saint (The Hawke Family - Book Five)

He's searching for absolution. She wants her happily ever after.

Solomon Clarke goes by Saint, though he's anything but. After lusting for him from afar, the masquerade party affords me the anonymity to pursue that attraction without worrying about the fall-out of hooking-up with the bouncer from the Hawkeye Club. From the second he lays his eyes and hands on me, I'm helpless to resist him. Even burying myself in a dangerous investigation can't erase the memory of our combustible connection and one night together. The only problem... he has no idea who I am.

Caroline Brooks thinks I don't see her watching me, the way her eyes rake over me with appreciation. But I've noticed, and the party is the perfect opportunity to unleash the desire I've kept reined in for so damn long. It also sets off a series of events no one sees coming. Events that leave those I love hurting because of my failures. While the guilt eats away at my soul, Caroline continues to weigh on my heart. That woman may be the death of me, but oh, what a way to go.

Life isn't always clean, and sometimes, it takes a saint to do the dirty work.

AVAILABLE AT ALL RETAILERS:

books2read.com/TaintedSaint

Steele Resolve (The Hawke Family - Book Six)

For one man, power is king. For the other, loyalty reigns.

Mob boss Luca "Steele" Abello isn't just dangerous—he's lethal. A master manipulator, liar, and user, no one should trust a word that comes out of his mouth. Yet, I can't get him out of my head. The time we spent together before I knew his true identity is seared into my brain. His touch. His voice. They haunt my every waking hour and occupy my dreams. So does my guilt. I'm literally sleeping with the enemy and betraying the only family I've ever had. When I come clean, it will be the end of me.

Byron Harris is a distraction I can't afford. I never should have let it go beyond that first night, but I couldn't stay away. Even when I learned who he was, when the *only* option was to end things, I kept going back, risking his life and mine to continue our indiscretion. The truth of what I am could get us both killed, but being with the man who's such an integral part of the Hawke family is even more terrifying. The only people I've ever cared about are on opposing sides, and I'm the rift that could end their friendship forever.

Love is a battlefield isn't just a saying. For some, it's a reality.

AVAILABLE AT ALL RETAILERS:

books2read.com/SteeleResolve

The Deadliest Sin Series (Dark Romance)

WRATH (Book One)

All I see is red.

Blood.

Pain.

Rage.

It consumes me.

The moment he took her, wrath invaded my soul.

I only have one purpose.

End him and take back what's mine.

Love isn't always clean, and wrath is the deadliest sin.

AFTER WRATH (Book Two)

They took something from me.

Something that can never be replaced.

They destroyed something.

Something that can never be repaired.

Only one thing can appease the burning rage in my soul.

Unleashing my wrath on those responsible.

The Dragon will rise.

Death will reign.

Because wrath is the deadliest sin.

SURVIVING WRATH (Book Three)

I fled into the night and didn't look back.

I grieved.

I loved.

Then he appears.

Dark.

Dangerous.

I never thought wrath would find me again.

But you can't run from it.

Not when wrath is the deadliest sin

The Slip Series (Romantic Comedy)

Dickslip (A Scandalous Slip Story #1)

One wardrobe malfunction. Two lives forever changed.

Playing in a star-studded charity basketball game should be fun, and it is, until I literally go balls out to show up my arch nemesis. When I dive for the basketball and my junk slips out of my gym shorts, I know my life and career are over. There's no way the network can keep my kids' show on the air after I've exposed myself to millions of people. I don't know how Andy, the new CEO, can go to bat for me with such passion. I also never anticipate how hot she looks in a pair of high heels.

Rafe's dickslip has made my new job even more stressful. It's hard enough being a woman in a man's world without dealing with sex organs being publicly displayed when someone is representing the company. But he's an asset to the network, not to mention hot as hell. I can barely keep my eyes off him or his crotch during our meetings. Defending him to the board puts my ass on the line as much as his, but it's worth it. So is risking my job to fulfill the fantasies I've had about him since he first set foot in my office.

Things may have started out bad, but… some accidents have happy endings.

AVAILABLE AT ALL RETAILERS:

www.Books2read.com/Dickslip

Nipslip (A Scandalous Slip Story #2)

One nipple. A world of problems.

I own the runway. Until my nipple pops out of my dress during New York Fashion Week and it suddenly owns me. Being called a worthless gutter slut by a fuming designer is the least of my problems. My career is swirling around the toilet like the other models' lunches. Until smoking hot Tate Decker steps in with a crazy idea about how his magazine can maybe salvage my livelihood.

It's less than two feet in front of me. Perfect and perky and pink. And the woman it's attached to looks absolutely horrified. I need to help her, and not just because she's beautiful and has a perfect rack. Using my position in the industry to expose the volatile nature of our business puts my career in jeopardy in an attempt to save Riley's. I'm willing to risk that, but falling for her isn't part of the plan.

When love and tits are involved... Things can get slippery.

AVAILABLE AT ALL RETAILERS:

www.Books2read.com/Nipslip

Beaver Blunder (A Scandalous Slip Story #3)

One brief mistake. A world of hurt.

No panties. No problem. At least until I slip on the wet floor and go heels over head in front of my colleagues and half the courthouse. Returning to consciousness can't be more awkward, until I find out who my sexy, argumentative, and bossy knight in shining armor really is. My career may not survive my beaver blunder, and my heart might not survive Owen Grant.

Madeline Ryan tumbles into my life on a wave of perfume and public embarrassment. She falls and exposes herself in front of me, and I find myself falling for her despite the fact she fights me every chance she gets. Being a woman in a good ol' boy profession demands a certain brashness, but it definitely has me thinking, maybe litigators shouldn't be lovers.

With stressful jobs and big attitudes, going commando has never been so freeing.

AVAILABLE AT ALL RETAILERS:

www.Books2read.com/BeaverBlunder